Another Morocco

D1157818

Published by Semiotext(e)
PO BOX 629, South Pasadena, CA 91031
www.semiotexte.com

"Turning 30" was translated by Daniel Simon and first appeared in *World Literature Today* in 2013,

"The Wounded Man" was translated by Frank Stock and first appeared in *Life As We Show It: Writing on Film*, edited by Masha Tupitsyn and Brian Pera, City Lights Publishers (2009)

Thanks to Noura Wedell.

Cover Photograph by Hicham Gardaf.
http://www.hichamgardaf.com

Design: Hedi El Kholti
ISBN: 978-1-58435-194-8

Another Morocco

Selected Stories

Abdellah Taïa

Translated by Rachael Small

semiotext(e)

Contents

To M'barka

1.

A Year at the Bibliothèque Générale

The first year of my life was spent in a library. And not just any library—it was the greatest and most prestigious, the one that held the entire archives of Moroccan History in its bowels, a place all researchers must visit eventually—the *Bibliothèque Générale* of Rabat.

Because my father, Mohammed, had worked there for a long time as a lowly public servant, and because he was helpful and kind, they'd allowed him to live rent-free in a little house in the garden behind the library. He might have also been a night guard. No, that's not right, that job went to Merzougue. Merzougue, the enormous black man with the red fez.

By the time I was born, my family had already been living there for three years. My mother, M'Barka, hadn't wanted another pregnancy, fearing she'd give birth to yet another girl. My brother Abdelkebir, the oldest, the favorite, was surrounded by girls, six sisters whom I loved even before I was born. He was a student at Moulay-Youssef High School and already had his first bicycle. Khadija, Rashida, Latifa, and Fatima were all educated—with varying degrees of success. Najat was five years old and Rabia was three. The family's closest friend was El-hajj El-Adaoui, a respected and highly esteemed theologian. An alim.

He was the one who chose my name. Abdellah: Servant of God.

Of course I don't remember anything from that first year—I was too young. All the stories I have to tell come from my parents, my sisters. They lived my life for me, recording it in their memory for a later time. Through them, I am able to relive it in snippets. As the newest arrival (this wouldn't last very long : three years later, Mustapha would show up to compete, though he never fully eclipsed me), I was spoiled, the center of attention, the most important person in the family, adored. Their pride. For many reasons, but mostly due to my sex: male. They'd spent so many years hoping I would come. But I was oversensitive, scrawny, and sickly. I needed constant attention. And I had it.

My father would take breaks from work to come see me, take me in his arms, relieve my mother of her duties—she always had too much to do. He'd play with me, tickle my tummy, bring me right up to his face and cover me in big kisses. He kept a close watch on my health and did everything in his power to ensure that I would want for nothing, that I would grow up to be a great man, worthy of my godfather El-hajj El-Adaoui. "My little bird, my little boy, someday you will be big and handsome. The whole world will be yours, my darling son. May god protect you…" And he would read suras from the Koran, running his right hand, always the right, first over my head, then over the rest of my little red and blue body. He did this to protect me from the evil eye of envy, from his brother, who had mocked him each time M'Barka gave him a girl. "Now, finally, he'll have to stop teasing me. No more pretending he's better. Thanks to you, little one. You've saved me… He used to come here and laugh at me, talking about his four sons, going on and on about them. Even his daughters were sons, to hear him speak of them. I was so ashamed. I couldn't go back to the village, all they ever asked about were my daughters, my six daughters, and no one ever even mentioned Abdelkebir… They would cruelly mock me: 'How will you ever marry off all your daughters? Poor Mohammed!' Over and over they'd say: 'M'Barka has brought you nothing but bad luck, failure. Leave her.' They made fun of me to my face and behind my back. But now I have two, yes, two fine sons. I can proudly return to the village. Go back and claim my share of the year's harvest. My brother can't steal it anymore. I have to pull myself together. Next summer, in just four months, I'll go with my head held high and demand what he owes me. He'll bring out his long monologue on my origins, but I won't give up. And it's all for you, my Abdellah. I'll do everything I can to make sure that you're better than all his sons and daughters. You'll go to school, to middle-school, to university… I'll bring myself to ruin to realize this dream."

Massaouda, my father's free-spirited sister, would come to stay with us from time to time, sporadically, even though she and my mother never got along. Despite her lack of love for my aunt, M'Barka would let her watch me. ("She won't hurt her brother's child.") I was her blood, the son she never had. I've always adored my aunt, probably because I spent so many hours on her knee that first year. Though I was just a baby, she would tell me stories, fabulous stories about runaways, travelers, starving animals, idiots, tricksters, djinns, people of God and the devil's people. She was the one who introduced me to the legends of our ancestors from Ouled Brahim.

Massouda's tales cradled my childhood, nourished me as much as M'Barka's milk.

I had been expected. They expected a lot of me. But I didn't know it. And so, as if to test their love, I often fell ill, seriously ill: intestinal problems. It was true that they really loved me. To heal me, my father would borrow money from many of his friends, his loved ones, from El-hajj El-Adaoui who always refused to be reimbursed, and never from his brother, his rival.

They expected me: keeping me cost them dearly. They sacrificed themselves for me. I was ill for about six of the first twelve months of my life. My body already eluded me, didn't do as it was told, didn't listen. As time went by, it would only get worse.

When I was more or less recovered, Mohammed would take me on tours of his Bibliothèque Générale. Holding me in his arms, so close to his chest, he'd walk among the bookshelves, infinite shelves, shelves that simultaneously ascended and descended. Later, he'd confess that he'd done this to accustom me to the scent of books, old books. He wanted to let their magical, unique and universal perfumes make their way into my mind and my senses. He would open one of them, in Arabic (he didn't read much French) and read to me for just a few minutes. This didn't always go smoothly—sometimes I cried. My cries would echo from room to room until they reached my mother, who would come running, alarmed, to my aid. I couldn't handle that much culture; I'd had more than my dose.

Merzougue, the enormous black man with the red fez, lived at the library too, but by himself. His wife had gone back to their village because she didn't speak a word of Arabic. He frightened me, or rather his skin did. Whenever I caught sight of it, I would wince in fear and scream as loud and as long as I could. Shrill cries that mobilized every member of my family. I must have hurt him, poor Merzougue, I surely injured him. Still, he never got angry with me, he had a big heart and no children of his own. He was the one who planned my first birthday party, bought the fruit, dates, dried figs, almonds, peanuts, orange blossom cakes, and many other things.

This was all heaped on my head, gently, slowly. And they ate all of it as they prayed for me.

It was a hectic year, full of happiness, recklessness, and problems. A year lived in my honor, which would later be shared with me as each member of my family offered up a little piece of myself. It was clear that I was loved.

But was I told everything?

2.

My Circumcision

My parents didn't decide to circumcise me until I was six, a year before I started elementary school. I remember everything. First and most of all, I remember my jealousy. My parents had decided that I would share the celebration with my little brother Mustapha. We would be circumcised together, at the same time. I hated the idea but didn't say a thing. I believed deep down that the celebration was mine, just for me. Incidentally, no matter how hard I try I can't recall any images of Mustapha during the big event. And what an event it was. Both sides of our enormous extended family came in for the occasion. Even those we didn't like, those with whom we had unfinished business were there—neighbors too, but not all of them. As usual, my mother was upset with several women in our neighborhood. Preparations began long before the party. They'd bought me a white djellaba and foukia, a holy-green embroidered tarbouche and yellow slippers—Mustapha was entitled to the same, I guess. A week before the happy day, my father went to a souk far away from our house and came home with a big cow. Our neighbors began to whisper: where had they gotten the money to buy a cow like that? Even I didn't know. They were jealous; they watched us too closely. Because she sensed this, my mother burned incense, fassoukh, and other things to protect us, so nothing would go wrong. She'd even asked the fkih of our mosque to make amulets that we had to wear all the time. At last, the weekend of the big event arrived. Everything was in place, or nearly.

Friday
Only our closest relatives had shown up, which meant many people, about thirty. They finished grinding the spices, putting cakes in the oven and cleaning, making sure everything was immaculate. The house was filled with unusual scents, but one that I truly loved over-powered all the rest—the scent of orange blossom water. M'Barka had bought liters and liters of it. Naturally, it's the water of baraka.

Tamou, the hajja, the best cook in all of Hay Salam, had brought all her materials into our yard where there was no risk of being disturbed. This was her one requirement: she must be left to work in peace. "To cook," she'd often say, "your mind must be peaceful. If not, it's impossible to concentrate, to create." With all she had to do, she really did need concentration. She also needed encouragement, which my mother would stick around to give her from time to time. That's how it was: we had to give her space, but couldn't abandon her.

After Al-Asr, around four p.m., the never-ending henna ceremony began. Just on the hands for me (Mustapha too, I think). For M'Barka, hands and feet. Circumcision is also a celebration of the mother—she too gets special treatment, almost like a new bride. This idea I was willing to accept, but the thought of sharing the spotlight with Mustapha was too much for me to bear.

We were surrounded by women, women who spoke, sang, shouted youyous, who pampered us and, as soon as they finished applying our henna, happily divided what was left among them-selves. This is said to bring luck. The henna of the innocents.

At nightfall, we were left with the men. Off to the hamam to purify our bodies and prepare to become men ourselves once we were clean, washed of all contamination.

I have no memories of that part, not even of myself.

Saturday

I was like a prince—they'd dressed me like one, enveloped me in perfume, nearly covered me in makeup (they'd cleaned my teeth with miswak, which made my lips quite red, and put kohl on my eyelids). They treated me like a girl. I had everything I wanted, candy, more candy… They kept hugging me, playing with me, touching my hair. For once, I was the one who had the baraka. It was glorious. And God knows I took advantage of it…

I was the envy of all the cousins who were my age, both the boys and the girls. They watched me with eyes full of longing, jealousy. So I pretended to be generous and offered to share my presents, but not all of them. I kept the best, most expensive ones well hidden. We played together—I was the king and they indulged my every whim. I wonder now what Mustapha was doing the whole time.

In the afternoon, they let me sleep, rest up. The grownups took care of different chores. The house was bustling. Other scents predominated. That Saturday's party was reserved for the men and the tolbas, readers of the Koran. This was not the most exciting part: I didn't like the way the tolbas spoke the suras, reciting them instead of chanting—it was monolithic. Luckily, that reception ended fairly quickly, and the neighborhood musicians took over, delighting our close family friends. My mother had paid my sister Fatima to dance and liven up the party. She carried out her duty marvelously but it took her three days to recover from the effort.

By midnight I was already asleep. I knew, however, that another obligation awaited me. They woke me at three a.m.; we had to go to the mosque for the ziyara. I was wearing nothing but a foukia and couldn't fully wake up. They put babooshes on my feet and the tarbouche on my head. Mama—that's what I called Fatema, my paternal uncle's wife—carried me on her back.

Outside, many women were waiting, carrying large, lit candles like the ones that are found in the mausoleums of holy men. They sang loudly and danced swiftly. The procession moved off toward the Al-Badr mosque in the same spirit. Youyous, songs, laughter. We felt and expressed such intense joy. The whole neighborhood got up to watch our procession pass by. Fatema was flanked by my mother M'Barka and my aunt Massaouda: these three were the most important women in my family. When we arrived at the mosque, they made me get off Mama's back and walk around the mosque three times, giving the door three kisses each time I walked in front of it. In the end, they gave me a candle to light. All of this lasted about an hour. I was delighted but had just one desire: sleep.

For once the family seemed united, but only in appearance. Mama was actually M'Barka's worst enemy, but despite this fact, I would love her for as long as she lived. She'd always paid attention to me, showed me such affection. The feeling was mutual.

Sunday

I knew that they were going to pull the bird trick on me: look, look at that little bird in the sky, and oof! they'd snip off my foreskin. I knew it well. This scam had been pulled on every boy in the neighborhood who'd been circumcised before me, every single one. So I was expecting it. I wasn't afraid of the pain.

The hajjam arrived around ten o'clock, along with his two assistants. He was the most famous hajjam in all of Salé and had been named their dean. With him, everything went according to plan, no mishaps. And so it was with me. I felt no pain. I became a man easily, painlessly, without screaming, amid the youyous of all the women who watched the scene unfold, curious and attentive, smiling. Nothing escaped them.

A man—so easily?

Afterward, they placed me in M'Barka's lap where I would receive congratulations from all our guests and a shower of cash, big bills. I fell asleep fairly quickly. Paradise.

When I awoke in the afternoon I was in pain, so much pain. No, becoming a man is not that easy. I'd been wrong. Later, it would get even more difficult.

That night, I wasn't able to go to the women's party. They were more elegant than ever, dressed in caftans—or rather in takchitas—excessively made up, wearing too much perfume. I couldn't even move. What was the point of being a man?

3.

Our Radio

At first, our house in Hay Salam had only one floor. There were three rooms. One for my parents, the second for Abdelkebir (why did he get his own?) and the third for the rest of the family, all eight of us: my six sisters, my little brother Mustapha, and me. The rest of the house consisted of a kitchen that was neither large nor small, a patio, and a courtyard. And then of course there was the terrace, which in time would prove itself useful for many things: slaughtering the goat for Eid, hanging our clothes out to dry, playing house with girls, playing doctor with boys, listening to music on the tiny transistor radio we'd stolen from the souk, smoking cigarettes in secret, crying without getting caught, venting our fury in silent shouts, and spying on neighbors, etc.

We didn't own a television. All we had was an old radio that would be worth a fortune today. There's a famous photo of King Mohammed V listening to a radio—we had the same one. But ours was almost always breaking down, and when it seemed to be working it only played one station: the official RTM. I still know its programming schedule by heart. Every morning before nine, they announced the cultural programs. Then, for the next three hours, local radio stations would take over (I especially liked the one from Marrakesh). At noon the main station from Rabat would come back on. In the afternoon there was a very popular program, *The People's Place*, where they spoke openly about civil issues. In the evening we'd hear the Moroccan soap opera with Moroccan characters speaking Moroccan Arabic. This always surprised us and made us all very happy, especially M'Barka. We felt as though we were listening to ourselves speak. I'd read wonder on the faces of my family members, in their eyes. Suddenly we'd hear sentences (sometimes insults) that were part of our daily life pronounced, broadcast into the air, soaring high, so high. They entered through our ears to shake our minds and cloud them. It made us happy. We were transported, silently held captive beneath the radio's magic waves, unresisting. But every once in a while, something would snag. A word pronounced too classically or pretentiously would infuriate us. "Traitors! We don't speak like that. It sounds so fake."

The radio sat in the middle of the patio, atop the small cupboard where we kept the guest dishes. We put it on display so that all our guests would notice it the moment they arrived. It was without a doubt our most precious possession at the time and we showed it off accordingly. In the little corner next to it, we kept a disorganized collection of certain rare records: Sheikh Abdelbasset Abdessamad, the greatest Koranic chanter in the Arab world, Mohammed Abdelwahhab, Bouchaieb El-Bidaoui, who frequently dressed as a woman, and the popular singer Houcine Slaoui, whom I loved most of all. Slaoui, from Salé, like me. He dared to sing about love in a way that verged on obscenity but didn't disturb us. He was already dead by the time I was born but his songs were still very popular. His voice accompanied our evenings; his words enchanted us, made us laugh and reconciled us with life. He was a *bon vivant*, a man of pleasure. You could feel it, hear it. I would eventually learn that he began his career singing in cafés in Salé and that people—mostly men—came from far away just to see him. I've never seen his face. All I've ever had is his voice. I imagine him as a traditional man who wore a djellaba, a short, tidy beard, and a red tarbouche on his head—a thin man with brown skin, a real man who harbored his own mysteries. He had a secret life, in love with a waiter who worked at the café where he would perform, and who received all his affection and inspired his songs—a young houseboy, a teenager who loved to serve, to please and keep secrets buried deep within himself. And the women whose voices accompanied him? They were surely shikhats, indulgent dancers who understood.

I can still picture my whole family during those long evenings by the radio, each of us with our shoulders draped in blankets, scarves, or shawls. We huddled close together in a circle, passing energy and heat between us, especially in the winter. My father stayed in a corner, at a distance from the rest of the family, and Abdelkebir spread out on the bench in his room with the door open. My mother—always with us, in our circle—often held me on her lap. My sister Rashida would inspect my hair for lice. I was surrounded by women. Men were far, so far from my mind. Mustapha, the baby, would fall asleep quickly and I'd be left with no competition. I had my women, their affection, all to myself. They took care of me in turns, each according to her expertise.

We'd turn off the lights. Total darkness. Fear of the dark disappears when there is a voice to comfort us and capture our attention. The voices on the radio were highly suggestive, always alluding to love. A thwarted love, of course—between Wassila and Hisham, between Badia and Fouad, rich and poor, student and worker; all the possibilities were played out for our enjoyment.

Saying "I love you" is difficult. Uttering that sentence in the presence of one's father is unthinkable where I come from.

Hshouma, shame. Unfortunately, it came up fairly often in these radio shows. That was the signal: time to disperse, go to sleep and let your imagination fill in the rest, or at least try to. Sometimes, Mohammed would simply leave the patio. Other times, when he was angry, he shut off the radio completely, grumbling. "Infidels! These people are obscene and if you don't go to bed right away, you'll end up as shameless as they are. Go to bed and do it quietly." How strange, love exists only among infidels. It would be pointless to describe our frustration. Our radio love stories were suspended, condemned.

I think we are afraid of love in Morocco. We never directly express our feelings. Affection, on the other hand, is always present. It belongs to women.

In the summer, the radio became even more appealing. It stayed on all day (when it was in good health). This never failed to create tension and sometimes even spectacular fights (shouts, the shouts of the hamam). With eleven people sharing one roof as we did, such tensions are inevitable. But these frictions could show up suddenly, for other reasons. It really had nothing to do with the radio. That was just an excuse. Still, peace would return quickly and we'd crowd around the radio again, in the same sphere, in our regular circle and now nearly naked: our skin glistening, hot, damp and touching. We loved each other, without saying it.

Then one day Abdelkebir discovered another station, Midi 1. It broadcast programs from Tangier, a distant city where people spoke Spanish as well as Arabic. An alien station? Yes, of course. They spoke a wild language that we didn't understand. Only Abdelkebir and Rashida seemed to know it. I was shocked. How on earth had they learned it? And where? The language of those rich people who lived far away, who came to visit from time to time and then left without inviting us along. "So rude!" M'Barka would always respond, outraged. That language was French. We felt its power, its arrogance. We were struck by an unbearable feeling of inferiority whenever we heard it. We got our revenge. We rejected it.

The day the infidels' French entered our little house, our communion with the radio was lost forever. My father bought a television a little while later. It wasn't the same. It would never be the same.

Many years later, I looked for our much-vaunted radio. Gone for good. No explanation. Mystery. So I imagined it returned to its country of origin: Japan. Japan?

4.

The Companion

For a long time, I accompanied my mother and two of my sisters, Khadija and Fatima.

Khadija has always been married, as far back as I can remember. From the beginning, I associate her with Bouchaib, her kindly husband, the only man in the family other than Abdelkebir who had a moustache. They spent the first two years of their marriage living in our house, where Khadija gave birth to Mohammed, their first child. I helped raise him, took care of him while Khadija cleaned, carried him on my back and rocked him to sleep. I even told him stories, Aunt Massaouda's stories. He got used to me, to my voice, my scent, my little eight-year-old body. But I never changed his diapers. That was too disgusting.

Khadija is the only one of all my sisters who inherited my mother's regal carriage, her hair and her formidable personality. Like our mother, she would have nine children; like her, she would spend her life fighting. The years didn't wear those two out: they're still always prepared to fight for their rights, whatever it takes. But they never agreed. M'Barka and Khadija would fight over the slightest thing and then make up fifteen minutes later. I'll never understand the relationships between women—they're too complicated. My mother was infinitely tender with us boys. With her daughters, she was often strict, uncompromising—even jealous. Maybe I'm wrong. When Rabia wanted to get married, M'Barka didn't hesitate to speak her mind: she was against it. She wanted Rabia to work first, make a future for herself, have a bank account. "The husband comes later," she liked to say, "on his own, and if not, by force." Rabia went her own way. And in time, my mother was proven right. Now she reminds Rabia every chance she gets. In fact, aside from Abdelkebir, M'Barka has never had a say in who her children married. She's never really accepted their husbands. She tolerates them.

But back to Khadija, whose husband may have been the only one my mother liked even slightly, and only just so. Why? Each weekend while they lived with us, he would bring home a basket full of meat, fruits, and vegetables. At that time, any gift was welcome. Those were our lean years. And so my mother thought Bouchaib was good, until she discovered his true colors.

When Khadija was bored or needed to take her son to the clinic for shots, Bouchaib would ask (or rather, order) me to accompany her. This meant that I had to skip class. Not a moment's hesitation—I was happy to do it. I can clearly remember the time I escorted her to the mausoleum of Sidi Ben Abdellah Ben Hassoun, the holy man, famous for calming rabid children. After walking seven times around the saint's tomb, as they do in Mecca around the Kaaba, I helped my sister place her son on the sill of the mausoleum's magical window, which provided blessings, I was told. Then we visited the caretaker of the holy place, the sharifa, who traced Mohammed's face with an egg a number of times before hammering a nail into the wall just above his head.

We finished earlier than expected, before the third prayer of the day, al-Asr.

"Want to go to the beach?" Khadija suggested. "It's so close by."

And it was. The Salé city beach was a ten-minute walk from the mausoleum. Khadija was the one who wanted to see the sea, even more than I did. I played the role of the child.

"Oh, yes!" I answered. "Yes please, let's go!"

"Ok, ok. But only if you promise not to tell anyone, not M'Barka, not Bouchaib. Promise?"

"Yes, yes, I promise!"

It was May, and it was hot. The beach was full of soccer players and students preparing for their exams. I saw the sea for the first time in my life. I was eight years old. In second grade. First in my class, which guaranteed that I would have the teacher's trust and affection for the whole year. Want to insult me? Easy: call me girly. I did seem a bit girly, even to myself—very girly according to the other kids. For me, the world had only one name: Salé, my city.

The scent of the sea, of the ocean, an awakening, beckoning scent that will always be within me, in my veins, my heart, my soul; the smell and the waves that come quickly, one after the other, and create such a delicious sound, never monotonous, a sound that is different each time, that swept me away, entered through every pore, and plunged deep into my body. They are still there.

We were sitting on the sand, facing the sea. In front of us, a bit to the left, stood the Kasbah of the Udayas, which protected Rabat and taunted Salé. Khadija took off her green scarf but kept her blue djellaba on. We stayed like this a long time, not saying a word, not doing a thing.

Living, we were truly living.

Fatima is the most modern of my sisters, the one with the greatest thirst for freedom. She set herself apart from the others early on. She had different dreams. European dreams, I believe. Dreams that shook her constantly. Staying at home, calm and obedient like a well-raised young lady, wasn't for her. She wanted to go out, to see other things. And so she did.

At first it was difficult. Every time, she was reminded that she was, above all, a girl. She made up all sorts of lies to get what she wanted: "I'm going to go study with Ilham." "I'm going to help Seoua and her mother bake cakes for her brother's wedding." "We have a make-up class this afternoon." Classic, nothing new at first. Then came the day when she no longer knew what to say, what excuses to make. She was at a loss, unhappy. Asking my other sisters for help? Pointless: they were from different worlds. And anyway, she never thought about it. She had other things on her mind.

"Abdellah, I've been invited to Radia's birthday party. Want to come with me?"

An interesting proposal. Completely unexpected. I didn't understand right away what she wanted from me.

"Sure, I'd love to," I responded, smiling, delighted.

"I'll tell M'Barka."

The latter agreed, "but only because Abdellah's going with you. He'll take good care of you." M'Barka was counting on me. Her mistake. As soon as Fatima and I left the house, we separated, went our own ways, with plans to meet up at the end of the day and return home together. This scenario was repeated successfully many times. I would go to Imade the Asthmatic's house, or to see Oussama the Brilliant. As for Fatima, I had no idea where she went or with whom. When we met again, at dusk, for the rest of our script, she was always happy, so happy. That's wonderful, I thought, unaware of the source of this happiness. I would grow to understand. Her face shone with love, she lived for love. So love made people happy, light. I promised myself that I too would fall in love.

Our games ended the day Fatima found me in an intimate, embarrassing position. I was in a state of ecstasy. And not alone.

As the years went by, she actually did gain her freedom. No one reprimanded her anymore. She did what she wanted fearlessly. My mother had washed her hands of her. One day, in anger, Fatima shouted at our mother, "You've never loved me. All you think about are your sons. You don't care about me. My life doesn't matter to you, I don't exist. You're not my mother anymore." To which M'Barka responded, ironically, "But you're the one who wanted to be free; you told everyone to stay out of your business."

M'Barka and Fatima never worked things out. Fatima and I have one thing in common: French literature, which we both studied at the university. We chose the culture of the nonbelievers. My mother saw this as a betrayal.

Fatima, as she aged, became more traditional—though not entirely so. She got married and recently had a child. I can't imagine her as a mother, but it seems she's okay at it. Life's strange.

M'Barka is peerless, but also just like all Moroccan mothers. Sweet, violent, unpredictable and surprisingly strong. She has a gift for leading others, guiding them, forcing them to bend to her will. She knows what to say to get what she wants. When she wanted water, she'd say: "My dear, bring me a glass of water, I'm thirsty. Your beloved mother who carried you nine months in her belly and raised you is thirsty. Go, go find a glass of water. May Allah open the gates of paradise for you and let you drink water from the well of Mecca, Zamzam." How could anyone not want to satisfy such a minor request when it's accompanied by all those entreaties, when it's the very guarantee of your salvation, even? One would have to be completely heartless to refuse her. Sometimes, though, I'd say no. Such prayers, after hearing them all day long, begin to lose their meaning: we stop hearing them or paying attention to what they entail, what they might bring us. We become blind, deaf. Not for very long, fortunately. One day, we'll miss those entreaties, and there will be nobody to walk us to the door whenever we leave the house, with her prayers and promises for the future. Nobody to say, with such feeling, "Go, go, I won't close the door right away. May Allah open the world to you; go, go, my ancestors will accompany you, they'll light your way." Nobody. And we're alone. Nobody to make the simple request, "May Allah go with you with His goodness and His mercy; come to the souk with me and help carry my basket." I did that, too.

In Hay Salam, the neighborhood of Salé where I lived, there are two souks: the one we call Douar El-Hajj Mohammed, the closest, and the one with the strange name, Souk El-Kelb, because it is rumored that the butchers sell dog meat and pass it off as lamb— that market is the farthest away from us and the cheapest. We would normally go there to run our weekly errands.

M'Barka and I love each other, with much more than the love between a mother and son. I can never say no to her, or almost never. I would go with her to both markets, even if it didn't always please me. And when I really didn't want to, she would even bribe me in her own way: "If you come with me, I'll buy you bananas." That's my weakness. I love bananas! We would walk side-by-side among the stalls; she was so lovely in her sky blue djellaba. I was always struck by a feeling, which would sometimes make me uncomfortable, a feeling that I was not M'Barka's son but her husband.

M'Barka gladly took me with her to see the holy marabouts or the fortune teller whom she'd visit from time to time, a kindly seer who worked with good djinns. Her name was Salha, and she liked me a lot. When M'Barka was invited to a wedding or baptism, she would bring me with her to celebrate with the women. She never left me with my father, to go with him to men's events. (But really, what is there to do in the company of men, heads of families? They're too serious about being men, showing off their virility. They desperately lack spontaneity and imagination. With women, each moment is theater, the circus, a spectacle of dancing, perfume, caftans, looks, jealousy, quarrels—things happen among them, between them, and you're never bored.) M'Barka even managed to bring me to the women's hamam (happiness in Hell) until I was six years old. After that, I was forced to join the men's side, where I was surprised to see them in a new light: fragile, sensitive, handsome, and open to all experiences. An infinite tenderness passed between their bodies, through their strongly scented, intoxicating skin. They brushed against each other, they touched. Pure sensuality. When I left the women's hamam, I began, little by little, to get closer to men and discover their feminine side which they would try, more or less successfully, to cover up. Mine is more visible: I need it to live.

For a long time, I accompanied women. Now, they are the ones who accompany me.

5.

The Majmar

Winter. No heating in our home in Hay Salam. All season long, we'd wear more layers inside that house—so unlike the others, the setting of all the main events, great and small, of my Moroccan life—than we would when we went outdoors.

At night, we all knew what pleasures awaited us. We came home quickly—some from work (my father from his Bibliothèque Générale and my sister Latifa from the company where she made rugs: a najjaja), some from school or university (my brothers, my other sisters and myself). My mother and sister Najat would light a fire in the majmar with coals bought from Soussi Hassan. We stayed in the same room, around our little glowing majmar. One by one, we'd warm our hands, feet, arms, even faces. We would bump into each other. We burned. We were drawn to this sole source of light, emanating from the embers, a blazing, branding, hypnotic light. Once settled in beside the glowing majmar, it was hard to leave. And then there were the sounds of the fire, its language, its monologue, its tantrums…

Dinnertime came, and we'd heat our food on the majmar as well. We mostly ate (cheap) starchy foods, usually fava beans, in the winter. After that, we'd make mint tea—our dessert. While we sipped it slowly, someone would begin to talk (no surprise, it was usually M'Barka) and tell tales. My father would sometimes use these moments to tell riveting religious tales (the life of the prophet Mohammed and his apostles). Finally, we would move the majmar into a corner of the room, for if we huddled around it too long we'd get headaches. We would bring it out to the courtyard before bedtime so it could also go to sleep and quickly air out the room (to get rid of the carbon monoxide, we remembered how our Berber neighbors' two sons almost died because they forgot to take the majmar out of the bedroom). We would sleep nestled beside each other, finishing the stories we'd already begun so that we could begin telling others.

All winter long, our daily lives found meaning only in those long evenings we spent huddled around the majmar. We were poor. There wasn't much money in the house. It was utter misery. Quite obviously, I was fooling myself.

6.

The Military Pool

"Come on Abdellah. Grab your suit and follow me. The pool is open to everyone today. Don't stare… Hurry up!"

"But I don't have a bathing suit Mustapha, you know that."

"Then wear your black underwear, nobody'll notice… Come on, don't be a sissy. We have to go, they're waiting for us."

I couldn't believe it—the rich soldiers' pool was open to us poor kids! I couldn't believe it. But my little brother Mustapha was adamant and confident. He said he'd heard it from a credible source. I didn't believe it. Still, I put on my black underwear and followed him.

The military base wasn't far away. A fifteen minute walk at most, twenty in the summer because of the heat. I didn't know the families who lived there. Wealthy people. Their kids didn't go to our school. I saw them pass by in their chauffeur-driven cars. They were rich—they must have been, since they had chauffeurs. I didn't know what their houses looked like; they were hidden behind a very tall wall, kind of like a prison. But I believed that they must be palaces. I imagined these rich people were all very happy, peaceful, no shouting, no problems, a well-ordered life. Everyone had his own room, a maid too. They could only be happy. In the summer they had the pool. The same pool that they were sharing with us, suddenly with us, the dirty children of the masses.

During the twenty-minute walk, silent like the other boys, oddly, I dreamed. No ambitious dream (wooing some general's daughter). I merely saw myself in the pool's clean, cool water. I could see a happy me, playing with artificial waves almost naturally. It didn't take long for this image of serenity to be shaken by a cruel realization. Why hadn't I thought of it before? I didn't know how to swim. So where was I going? To humiliate myself in front of everybody, again? I had to turn around. I wasn't ready to handle the drama, and in the middle of the summer. But what excuse could I give? The other kids wouldn't let me go easily. Especially Mustapha.

Fear interrupted my dream of joy. Luckily, I remembered what my friend Imade once told me in middle school. He said that every pool had a part reserved for kids who didn't know how to swim. I was saved. Thank you Imade.

I was happy and dreaming again. Hot too.

A crowd had formed in front of the entrance to the base, a huge crowd.

"Do you think they'll let us all in?" I asked Mustapha.

"I don't know. But you and me, we gotta get to the other side. Forget about the others. We'll slip forward quietly and, as soon as that cocky guard lifts the gate, we'll rush through. Run if you have to. Got it? Answer me when I talk to you, don't be a wimp. You gotta fight for what you want. Follow me…"

I had no choice. He enjoyed calling the shots—making plans, executing them, playing seriously. But all that wasn't for me. I was happy to follow. The way I saw it, getting through the gate would be impossible. They couldn't let everyone in the pool, it would get dirty too quickly. Nope, impossible. Mustapha was still confident. He kept flashing signs at me. I imitated him and moved forward. And despite all my hesitation, I still firmly believed in my dream of water.

We couldn't go any further—we were at the front. We'd stay there an hour waiting under a merciless sky. Then another hour. And a deep discouragement finally set in. We returned home with wet eyes.

Before we split up, Mustapha and I and all our friends figured out how we'd get even. The next day, without telling our parents, we'd sneak off to the beach. The dream would live on.

7.

Bread and Tea

"One ticket please. It's five dirhams, right?"

"No. Today it's ten."

"Why?"

"What? You don't know? The second show is the new Amitabh Bachchan movie. It just came out in India last month."

"No, I didn't know. Who's Amitabh Bachchan?"

The man at the ticket counter, a forty years old with a nice, neat mustache, looked at me as if I came from another planet. No answer.

I was nine years old. I wasn't yet familiar with Amitabh Bachchan. I'd gone to the theater that Sunday to watch a Bruce Lee movie: *Return of the Dragon*.

The theater was plunged in complete darkness. Familiar Chinese music filled the air. The spectators' eyes were riveted to the screen, as if they were waiting for a miracle. Not a whisper. Someone was coming, from another world.

The usher came up to me. I handed her my ticket.

"Oh! Another zero."

"Sorry?"

"Go, down there, in front. Sit on the floor."

She didn't give me time to figure it out, let alone protest. She'd already left. Unable to see my way in the dense darkness, I moved forward like a blind man.

"Hey! Watch where you're going, asshole. Sit down right here. Theater's full."

The voice of a giant. I complied without a grumble.

Seated on the floor in that smoky room, amid unknown bodies that touched mine, I raised my eyes to the screen and there he was, big and silent, enigmatic, already bare-chested—it was him, Bruce Lee. I loved him right away.

In my neighborhood, Hay Salam, there were two groups: the followers of Jackie Chan and those of Bruce Lee. Every once in a while, "wars" broke out between them, wars worthy of their heroes' films.

For many months, I stayed neutral, chose neither one nor the other. Of course, I knew them quite well: their posters were everywhere. After a while, I'd had enough. I had to choose my camp: which side was I on? I was no longer happy with neutrality—things were too calm and I was excluded from the neighborhood games. I couldn't stand the idea of being banished or excluded.

After unsuccessfully begging and begging my older brother Abdelkebir to take me to a karate or kung-fu movie with Bruce Lee or Jackie Chan, I decided to go by myself, like a big kid: after all, I was nine. The money was easy to get: I helped my mother run errands for a week and she gave me two dirhams a day in exchange. I made a total of fourteen dirhams. The Opéra movie theater was pretty far away, in the Tabriket neighborhood, but that didn't stop me. I'd made up my mind and I wasn't even afraid when my neighborhood friends told me that the movie theater was a regular hangout for the riffraff of Salé, rough guys, ruthless—I would keep as low a profile as possible.

Bruce Lee didn't speak much. He was effective and his movements were extraordinarily agile; he struck swiftly and kept his cool no matter what happened. He was a master of martial arts but it didn't go to his head. He was still humble, modest. When you saw him walking along in the streets or quietly working in a store, you'd never guess that he was so talented. He was that discreet. The hidden strength, that's what fascinated me. And he was always the Good guy, ready to help the poor, to rescue, to fight. All he ever needed were his hands and feet. He knew how to use them intelligently, without weapons.

Bruce Lee was everything a hero should be.

Without ever having seen a single Jackie Chan movie (I boycotted them for a long time actually), I took the side of my childhood hero: Bruce Lee, the Little Dragon.

This was the birth of my passion for kung-fu movies. I must have watched hundreds of them. They were all alike, but that never spoiled the pleasure of reaching the end—after many adventures, "Good" triumphs and the hero walks off victorious and alone. As for the training scenes, the neighborhood kids fully dissected them; we got deeply into them, imitating each movement or at least trying. I'll admit, I was the least talented; as soon as I started to move they all burst out laughing. I was ridiculous but I owned it. I couldn't care less, as long as I was part of a group, a clan, not rejected, living for a common passion.

One day the unthinkable happened. Someone in our clan brought us incredible news: Bruce Lee and Jackie Chan had made a feature film together and this movie was called *Brother Against Brother.*

We were shocked. Really? Master Bruce Lee and his little student in the same movie? Impossible! How could he lower himself like that and agree to share top billing with Jackie Chan who, according to all the neighborhood specialists, was much less talented. We were all outraged, furious.

Would we still go see the movie when it came out? Nobody would weigh in. So we decided to hold a conference the next day to make our decision.

At the agreed upon hour, the majority of clan members were absent. Only three of us had honored the meeting (Adil the lefty, Samir the liar, and me). We waited a while in silence, speechless. And then Samir blurted out:

"Hey! I thought I was the liar…"

We burst into nervous laughter. And we all set off for the theater to see a karate movie. We were convinced that our association was all over. From that moment on it would be each boy for himself. That wouldn't be too bad. But that day my friendships with the other boys began to change, while my relationships with Adil and Samir only got stronger.

The movie that Bruce Lee and Jackie Chan starred in together never came to Salé. I'm still not sure if such a movie was ever made. I stayed faithful to Bruce Lee.

Karate movies were always screened as double features before Indian films, which always seemed endlessly long. Every movie buff in Salé, and maybe in all of Morocco, knew about this arrangement and it became known as "bread and tea." People of my social class, commoners, couldn't imagine having one without the other. So instead of saying, "I'm going to see a karate movie and an Indian movie," we were more likely to say, "I'm going to see bread and tea." The bread was the karate movie. Tea, which we always drink with lots of sugar in Morocco, corresponded to the saccharine films that came from India.

I didn't like them. Girly movies. Too sentimental. Too sappy, too sweet. I'd leave in the middle, unable to stand the endlessly repetitious storylines any longer. Don't even get me started on the songs… The whole thing was intolerably kitschy.

Then how did I come to change my mind? How did everything I once hated become appealing to me?

I fell into the trap the day the tea was called *Sadaka*. I decided to stay until the very end for one reason: the movie had been dubbed in Moroccan Arabic. It was a memorable experience: I laughed like I'd never laughed before and even though the story was like all the others, time just flew by. From that point on, I had bread and tea like everyone else; it really is hard to swallow bread without a drink to wash it down.

After a while, I became an expert on Indian cinema. Amitabh Bachchan was, of course, the greatest. As for the actresses, to my friends' disdain I ardently defended the spiritual Chabana Azmi—the rest of them were simply robotic. What's more, I even learned some of the songs by heart. And when the hero finally got his revenge (all Indian movies are constructed around revenge) and at last found his mother, who had never stopped waiting and praying for him, I would cheer happily.

Thus the world would be saved twice in a row, in a single afternoon, first by a Chinese man, then by an Indian. We could go to sleep soundly. Order was restored and peace could reign once more, until the next showing a week later.

In 1984, Steven Spielberg's *E.T.* came to Rabat. Abdelkebir brought us to see it, my little brother Mustapha and me. He didn't realize that with this gesture, he was opening another door in cinema for me, the door to Western films that would lead me to other encounters: Truffaut, Hitchcock, Renoir, Scorsese, and many more. My love of cinema shifted. I became unfaithful.

To this day, I've never brought up this old passion for karate and Indian movies with my Moroccan friends. I was ashamed. I was wrong.

8.

The Last Time

"Abdellah, can you go to our uncle El-Bouhali's house in Bettana and ask aunt Massaouda to come over next weekend?" Abdelkebir asked.

"No problem. My class ends at four. I'll go then."

"Don't tell mom. You know why…"

Yes, I knew why, but I didn't know the whole story. My uncle had kept his parents' inheritance all to himself. He took everything: the land, the money, even the yearly harvest. He gave nothing to Massaouda or Mohammed. This exclusion, his dictatorship, it's all still a mystery to me—especially since my father, the so-called ladies' man, never sued him. They were angry with each other; despite this, they would spend time together, see each other, share water, bread, and fancy meals. Still, from time to time my father would cry. "What did I do to him to make him treat me like this?" he'd ask, "To make me the laughing stock of the whole village?" He would protest, and yet whenever El-Bouhali brought his family over to our house, my father would put himself deeper in debt to welcome him. He loved him in spite of everything. He loved him because he was his only brother, his other half, his blood, his past, his future—because he was like him, made like him. Because he was all he had.

Massaouda, who had never married, lived with El-Bouhali. She would visit us about once a month. She and Mohammed were very close, much closer than she was with her other brother. "She knows everything," M'Barka would say. "She could save your father if she wanted. She's the oldest, the first born. She's seen and heard it all. She's a fount of knowledge, but she's afraid that the other one will kick her out. Where would she go? If she wanted, she could come live with us, but she never will… Let her stay in the qahra!"

All of us adored Massaouda, beginning with Abdelkebir, who'd sent me to my uncle's house that day to ask her to spend a few days with us. He was afraid she might be ill, that her weak legs had given out.

My aunt wasn't ill. She was doing quite well in her old age, with her daily aches and simple pleasures. It was another woman in my uncle's house, a younger woman, barely fifty years old, who was bedridden. His wife: Fatema. We'd heard people talking about it in Hay Salam. "She never leaves her bed," said someone on my mom's side of the family who also lived in Bettana. She'd added—I remember this quite well—with a mixture of pity and frankness, "Allah is taking his revenge on her for all she's done to you. Allah is great. He never forgets." What had she done to us? Was this woman really talking about Fatema, the woman I affectionately called Mama? "Yes, yes," M'Barka responded, and told me about all the horrifying things Fatema had done, her offences, her hypocrisy, her sadism, her greed, her voracious appetite.

I couldn't recognize Mama in these images, they didn't fit with the ones I already had, all my wonderful memories of Fatema. Was it possible? Did she love me and hate my family? Declare her love for me and, in the same breath, wish me ill? Want me to live and die? Want to nourish and poison me? My heart couldn't accept all the things they said about her, and although M'Barka would later show me proof, my heart preferred not to see, to persist instead in its own truth. It would remain innocent, young, barely fourteen years old. It didn't want to lose the feeling of Fatema carrying Abdellah on her back on the night before his circumcision for the ziyara to the mosque. Other women had been present, but my heart could only remember Fatema. Curvy, plump, gentle Fatema, the Fatema who was proud of me, Fatema my Mama, my second mother. It hadn't seemed as though she had been acting or lying that night. The joy I felt before the pain of the circumcision was tied to her. Without her, it wouldn't have existed. It would have been impossible.

When I got to my uncle's house, my head was full of memories. I was perplexed, happy to go where I was forbidden. Afraid. Brave. I went inside. I could never have imagined what was waiting there for me.

The house was bathed in the scent of mint tea, which someone was preparing. There was another equally delicious smell, the smell of crêpes that had already been made and were ready to eat, elegant crêpes we called rozzet el-kadi (the judge's turban). I went inside and was struck by the feeling that I'd been expected, that they'd made an effort to welcome me, that someone had glimpsed me from afar and announced my arrival. Unless they had smelled me coming closer and closer. (When I was about to leave, Massaouda told me, "I knew you were coming. I had a dream about you and Abdelkebir while I was napping.") I went inside and everyone was there in the little, cheerless sitting room with its red seats. El-Bouhali was thin, yellow, sitting with his back hunched, oddly tender. Massaouda sat on the ground with her hand on her right cheek; her head was big and her face wrinkled—she had such beautiful wrinkles, the kind of wrinkles I'd like to have when I get old. She was thinking. Rquia looked as crazy as ever. Mina had strange eyes that could seem possessed. I entered and from the bathroom emerged a disfigured woman, an abandoned woman, a woman who had once been beautiful. I didn't know this woman. I didn't know her and yet, when she saw me, she opened her arms, inviting me to come close to her, nestle in to her, let her hug me and love me. She said my name twice, with difficulty, and I recognized her: it was Fatema, Mama. She tried to say my name a third time as she walked toward me, her eyes full of tears. She: "Oueldi, habibi, I've missed you so much." I: silence. What could I say? Silence. The silence of the end of the world.

She held me to her and hugged me tight, so so tight. I inhaled her scent, which I no longer recognized; it wasn't the same scent she once had. I touched her bones. She had nothing under her skin but bones, no more curves, no more fat. She seemed tiny to me, tiny and old at the same time. Her skin sagged. Her features reminded me of the walking dead in horror movies. Her white and yellow eyes, buried in a well, were not the eyes that had loved me so many times, that had transmitted thousands of messages of love.

She continued to hold me, didn't want to let go. Time no longer existed; none of the people around us existed. Only our two bodies, there in her courtyard, entwined. Two bodies that loved each other, and silence. The others didn't dare interrupt us, as though nervous, aware of the significance of the event. They left us in peace. That's exactly what it was, peace. God's peace surrounded us, guarded us, preserved us. Peace in our hearts and souls.

I was still inside her, now I was the one who didn't want to let go. I'd come to understand that Fatema was leaving. She was filling up on me before the big goodbye, taking a little piece of me with her for the voyage, for the other world. She was making up for things, asking me to forgive her. She repeated that word, whispered it in my ear. "Samahni..." Forgive her for what?

I found myself in another world with my heart tight. They spoiled and took care of me. Each of them, in their turn, voiced their strong feelings—each told me that they loved me, sometimes without words. In that dim, little room, we ate honeyed crêpes, a real treat, and drank glass after glass of mint tea. Only Fatema abstained since she couldn't eat everything anymore, the doctor had strictly forbidden certain dishes. I imagined her suffering, her misfortune. She'd developed a reputation as a great gourmand who would eat everything, even if she wasn't hungry, and spend hours and hours cooking dishes, making couscous. Now she watched us sadly in silence. She watched me in particular. She was crying, calling out to me, she was crying, I was crying. She was crying and smiling, toothless.

That's where it ends. I have no more memories, no images other than the ones I've just described.

A week later, Massaouda came to our house. She told us all about Fatema's misfortunes.

Fatema died in the village, far away. She wasn't even sixty years old. She left. I'm the last person in my family she saw before her final trip. One day, out of nowhere, I heard the news from Chouaib, one of her sons, my favorite cousin. "Nobody told you? She's with God now. She left us six months ago."

9.

The Scent of Paradise

"It has been like this from the beginning. Even as a child, you were sick all the time. First it was the intestines, yes, intestines... Yours are fragile, there were things you couldn't eat. I fed you only milk and your belly never deflated. I hoped from the bottom of my heart that, thanks to my milk, someday you would be as white as a Fassi, not brown like us. But you quickly turned yellow, even your eyes were yellow. I was afraid for you, afraid of jaundice, which had taken so many people from our village to the other world, the green world. It wasn't jaundice. You stayed yellow. They called you Yellow Abdellah.

"And then, once you began to leave the house, to run barefoot though I told you not to, to play soccer with Zeneib's sons, the sun was unkind to you. It didn't like your yellow hue—perhaps it saw you as competition. No, it never treated you kindly. It regularly attacked you. You'd fall. For five or six days, you wouldn't be able to lift your head. It gave you a horrible fever, a mad fever, the same fever that made El-Maâti into a majdoub, aimlessly wandering the streets. But he's apparently mabrouk: Hadda finally got pregnant simply because, for a month and three days, she fed him lunch. I couldn't imagine you as a majdoub. Unable to pronounce the words, I silently prayed for another fate, I almost wanted to create it. The fever lasted, without any sign of letting up. It was as if a bad djinn was living in you, a djinn you'd trampled underfoot without wanting to, injured unknowingly. It was taking its revenge on you, it became the sun's accomplice.

"Medicine would revive you. Medicine is expensive. But I had my own ways of curing you. It was my stepmother, the woman who replaced my mother in my father's bed and whose name I never wish to speak, who passed them on to me. Ways to cool a burning body, to drive off evil spirits, to control a man, to cast off spells, to smell the scent of paradise."

No, the sun had never been kind to me, it often punished me and deprived me of my health. Fever, fever. I saw another world, laying in my bed, dripping with sweat, my mother at my bedside. A world ruled the succubus Aisha Qandisha, who'd terrorized me as a child, queen of the shadows. I hurled so many insults at her, on her head, her breasts, her monstrous sex. I bothered her so many times as she did her laundry underground. She knew that she'd have a chance to get her revenge, torture me, beat me, call upon her invisible husband's secret army to use my body for target practice and besiege my brain with the worst of nightmares. Even as an adult, when I was in my twenties, she'd manage to return me to my childhood and its fears. Once more, the world would spin wildly around me, once more I'd scream without being heard, once more I'd spill hot tears that burned me but flowed within. I lived in hell, roasting as my aunt Massaouda called it.

Luckily, my mother was gifted and could show me heaven, make me smell it, briefly.

"I used to go into the woods and look for the crying trees, trees that bend down, that give of themselves willingly, that allow them-selves to be picked. Eucalyptus. I'd take a few branches with leaves that were still fresh, bright green in color, not dark green. I'd gather them from seven trees. I didn't deface these trees. I asked them as I picked, I asked permission: above all, you mustn't hurt them, ever. Guard their friendship, we'll always need them.

"After that, I'd visit the herbalist to buy henna, orange blossom water, as well as a few amulets to ward off the evil eye and undo the fasoukh's pestilence. I would never forget the jaoui, which gives off, when burned, a scent for which angels have a particular fondness.

"When I returned to the house, I'd crush the eucalyptus in the mortar, I'd add henna and in the end, I'd flood the mixture with orange blossom water. In this way, I created a scent that brought the spirit back to the body, a scent that opens the eyes and wards off all bad things. This is the blessed scent of paradise.

"Once the preparation was finished, I'd wrap your head in a blue scarf in which I'd put my sacred mixture. And I'd leave you alone like that, alone with God. Your face would quickly turn green, your pores would open up, and the battle would begin. I'd turn off the light and leave."

A cool, cool wind would fill my body, accompanied by a scent that matched coolness, an herbal scent, a scent that settled in to my body little by little. I knew this scent. It awoke my worries, my fears, it freed me and frightened me at the same time... I slept and didn't sleep. I remained very aware of the battle being fought between spirits in my body. The bad ones were strong, they wouldn't leave easily, they used all their power to raise my temperature, they shattered me, they spit on me. They filled me with horrifying images, blood everywhere, a knife that stabbed my heart and the feeling that I no longer existed, that I was done, that I believed myself lost, destined for God's hell. Still, I knew that the Prophet Mohammed—peace be with him—would save me. I was afraid. I was alone. I prayed mechanically, recited all the suras of the Koran I'd been taught at the msid. I resisted. I fought weakly.

This hell, this torture lasted an eternity. I watched the years pass, observed all the work of it, unable to speed up the process. It was an eternity that saw me constantly laid out in my bed, suffering, broken. Between life and death.

But soon, an ocean breeze would enter from the north, from above. Soon it would envelop me entirely and chase the disciples of Iblis back into the darkness. For it was Iblis, the most beautiful of angels, who led the attack. He was invisible, but I could feel his presence, his influence. The ocean breeze continued to free me, to support me. Iblis eventually drew back, followed by all those who worked for him: his wife, Aisha Qandisha and the bad djinns.

My fever would finally break. I was saved. At that moment, enormous doors like the ones in the Rabat medina would open before my eyes. Gardens everywhere. And above all, the scent of these gardens, the scent of paradise. I didn't recognize anything, everything was green, everything was new. Only the henna and eucalyptus were familiar to me. There were happy people, not many, people of a type that don't exist on earth. A magnificently handsome naked guard named Rayan. He asked me: "Do you observe Ramadan as you should, following all the rules?" I was preparing to answer, to lie. He added: "Don't lie, I'll know it." He inspired confidence in me: "I'm young, I'm only sixteen, I can't fast until the end, I'm not strong." So he recommended: "If you wish to be among the happy people you see playing and tasting joy someday, you must respect Ramadan. I'm the one who guides good fasters to heaven."

And I'd wake up. It was morning. My M'Barka had made semolina porridge. She looked at me, touched me, then opened the window and thanked God. Birds sang. I'd then tell her about my dream. She'd listen to me religiously. She understood me.

10.

Oussama

Whenever Oussama went to the hamam, it still showed two days later. His pale skin was still red and I was green with envy. His family wasn't from Fes or Rabat, and yet there was something distinguished about him, like a rich boy who wanted for nothing. And he was smart too. The proof: he wore glasses.

Oussama had everything I didn't. A stable family—the father, highly intellectual, a military judge; the mother, a cultured housewife and excellent cook, a refined woman anyone would want as a mother; two brothers and only one sister. They didn't have money problems. They seemed peaceful, happy.

Yes, I liked Oussama's family. How often I'd wish I could take his place, or at least be his brother and share his luck. I liked that family and I couldn't help hating them. My heart was in constant conflict, love and hate engaged in a ruthless war.

I met Oussama during our first year of middle school. Love at first sight. I was drawn to him and stared at him often, for long stretches of time, my mind full of questions. I could sense that he was smart, superior. His cheeks, which were always red, drove me crazy. I adored them. They made him look like a little Christian.

During that first year, he proved to be even smarter than I'd assumed. He was first in our class in every subject. He had it all. It would be ridiculous to say there was any competition between us. He was way ahead of me and I was no dunce. I did well on my exams, but not like Oussama. He didn't seem to do anything in particular, and yet he finished first in our class each term, almost effortlessly. There was no suspense: we knew from the beginning how it would turn out. I really admired him; I think I even idolized him. I wanted to spend my time with nobody but him, hoping that his baraka, his blessing, would rub off on me at least a tiny bit.

I never left his side—sat next to him in every class, followed him around during recess. I'd pick him up before school: "It's on the way. I don't mind." I left my house an hour early to be sure I could stay at his for at least fifteen minutes, spend fifteen minutes in his company, intensely. Breathing the air in his house, its distinct and delightful scent. It also gave me time to compare his home with mine. Of course, I didn't like anything about ours. Oussama's house, now that was more my style. I would have loved to live there and never leave, spend all my days in that house full of books, where everything was organized, where everything seemed magical. It was the house of my dreams. I was in a trance. I'd stop by every chance I got. I really must have bothered him, disturbed him though I didn't mean to. I took it too far, past the limits of friendship.

His mother liked me, I think. His father would say hello from time to time. Their intimacy fascinated me. I even took an interest in the walls that sheltered them. I touched them to examine them, to uncover their secrets.

Oussama had a young aunt on his mother's side who was in her twenties and very beautiful. A small brunette with magnificently black eyes, thin lips that were constantly smiling. She seemed like the ideal woman for my older brother, who was looking for a wife at the time. If I only had the power to join our two families, combine them, mix our blood, I would happily have done so. I spoke to Oussama about it and he responded, amused, "Stop dreaming, she's already engaged. She's getting married in a year." Cruel Oussama! She had a fantastic name: Badiaa. Badiaa, the woman my brother would never marry. Is she happy in her marriage now, still as beautiful and fresh as always?

In the first year of middle school, there was one biology teacher whom I deeply hated. She taught well enough. But she only had eyes for Oussama. She doted on him shamelessly in front of all the other students. She'd even caress his pink cheeks, to congratulate him on his good work supposedly. But it was obvious: that dry, bony old maid—that's what we called her—fantasized about little Oussama. And since she had authority over him, she took advantage of it. She had no right to do that. All the other students noticed this special treatment and took every chance they got to make fun of poor Oussama about it, to tease him mercilessly. He would blush deeper and deeper, to my great pleasure. Luckily, this teacher switched schools the following year. I don't even remember her name.

Over the next three years my passion for Oussama remained as intense as ever. But with time I learned to hide it, to keep my distance, suffer alone in silence. I learned to give him space. What's more, as I began gravitating toward literature, he moved toward the sciences. We separated. With age, you learn how to lie to yourself, to become reasonable: you reflect more, become less spontaneous. But, at least, thanks to this introspection, you get to know yourself better.

As for Oussama, I lost track of him for eight years. Three years ago, I found him again. And it all came back to me.

11.

An Afternoon with Sidi Fatah

I was sick. Nothing worked. Everything was closing in on me, all the doors, all the faces. My optimism, which provided for me, gave me patience, hope, expectations had suddenly abandoned me, leaving me alone in Rabat, far from my room, my refuge, far from Salé. I was in the darkness. Everything was obscure. Everything had lost its charm, its specificity, its color. Even so, early that afternoon I was brimming with vitality: my day had gone exactly as planned, classes at the university in the morning, lunch in one of that same university's parks with the sweet Saâdia (we often shared the sandwich my mother made for me each morning, an omelet with fries and onions. We grew tired of it at times, always eating the same thing, so we would dream...), afternoon at the French Cultural Center, and lingering in the evening, educating myself, clinging to dreams.

Since pleasures did not come to me of their own accord, I fabricated my own. I was the one who sought them out. I certainly had enough, but is enough enough when you're a dreamer, and ambitious too?

I was sick. My whole body had followed this sickness, indefinable as it was. It was as if my angels were no longer watching over me, as if I had lost my ancestors' baraka, as if I was withering. Sad, that's how an outside viewer would have judged me. But it was even worse than that: a terrible disorientation (I didn't know which path to follow). I wanted to cry but I couldn't. Destabilized. Afraid of remaining forever frozen, with unrealized dreams, dreamed dreams. The fear that leads to nothing, the fear that the things you have always believed in will get you nowhere. Fear which terrifies, which sticks to your skin.

The world stifled me.

I quickly left the French Cultural Center. I crossed the Avenue Mohammed V at full speed. I passed through the medina gate and hurried down countless narrow streets that brought me to the mausoleum of Saint Sidi Fatah.

I'd been thinking about my mother M'Barka when I had the idea to make the pilgrimage to Sidi Fatah. Whenever she wasn't feeling well, whenever she said that the world was strangling her, she went there to restore herself so she could breathe better, so that life would gleam again, so that she would be happy for herself and, consequently, for those around her.

Mausoleums of saints are ordinarily divided into two sections: a section for prayer, a sort of mosque in fact, and the tomb where mostly women go.

At the entrance of Sidi Fatah, I bought a candle. I had to bring him light, honor him in this way so that he would give me his baraka in return, his own light that is, which would guide me, help me to find my way, a light that burst forth from the darkness, from another world, a pure world, a light that would enter my body and chase off the sickness that had suddenly settled there.

After lighting the candle and placing it on the saint's tomb I circled it seven times. I prayed for him, I prayed for myself. I whispered brief suras from the Koran. I touched the green keswa that covered his tomb. Many women were doing what I was doing, or rather I imitated them, copying their gestures. They all seemed to be elsewhere, in their own universe. Each had something to ask of Sidi Fatah. Isn't he, after all, the one who opens doors, as his name suggest?

As I was completing this rite, I felt peace enter me, a still foggy peace, that was not completely defined. So I continued my ziyara. I wanted my whole heart to be touched by the baraka. I prayed fervently.

All around me, chatting, sat women, women whose spirituality I shared, with whom I was in communion. There were all kinds of women, old ladies in djellabas, young women in suits, women from the countryside who'd made the trip from very far away, rich women, poor ones. They mingled as they would never do any-where but here. They didn't judge each other, they shared looks of such kindness. They were sisters. And amid all of them was me, the only man, the only boy. They inspired confidence in me. They looked at me with welcoming eyes, inviting me in this way to stay with them, that we might all love each other together. I responded to their invitation.

A community of unhappy people who had nowhere to go, who had nobody to tell about their miseries, just this welcoming saint, this saint who relieves, who gives baraka.

I sat down near an old and beautiful woman, whose hair was still slightly dark.

"Come closer, my son. What's your name?"

"Abdellah, Lalla."

"What a beautiful name. You are close to our God. He is with you, He follows you, like He does us all. Tell me, what are you looking for here? It's rare to see young people like you in this mausoleum."

"I'm looking for peace… I want to see life with holy colors, white, green, not the blackness that suddenly seized me this afternoon. I don't like that color…"

"You mean that the candle that illuminates your soul has burnt out. Is this your first time coming here?"

"Yes…No… When I was little, I'd visit the saints with my mother, even for pilgrimages… and then, I don't know why, but I stopped… Anyway, this is the first time I've come here alone. Before, when I was sick, I would sleep, I would read. Today my footsteps have brought me here… I followed them. And I already feel peace returning, I'm breathing better. There's something special here, unique."

"Yes, this place is unique."

She came close to me, kissed me on the forehead, looked into my eyes, almost in tears. She pulled many colorful strings of prayer beads from the pockets of her djellaba, passed them over my head, my heart, my hands, uttering incantations that I was unable to decipher. She was overflowing with goodness. With love. She was giving, giving… And I received all of it. All the women looked at me.

I left an hour later. I went to the Moorish café inside the Kasbah of the Udayas, to have tea and contemplate the tide, the Ocean, the Bou Regreg River.

I returned home with a light heart. My mother had been waiting for me so we could eat the delicious crêpes that she made every afternoon. It was just the two of us, now that the house was empty. I told her about my ziyara.

12.

From One Body to Another

Because of this little body shivering with pleasure, approaching in the shadows of our neighborhood hamam where the lights are only lit after six p.m., summer and winter alike, because of this lovely, youthful body with skin as white as milk, as soft and as clean—only to the eye—as those of the "Nassrani," it was impossible for people not to notice. This luminous body outshone the artificial light. And it was true: it (the body) came into the hamam, it moved from one room to the next as it made its way toward the monstrous basin, clinging to its parent. And the men, the tough ones who wouldn't come to clean themselves, especially in this traditional bathhouse, without at least a verbal fight (when it was physical, it was even better, but sadly that didn't happen as often as it used to), fell silent. Some even interrupted the place's essential ritual; all forgot the light they'd been complaining about for a half-hour. They were hypnotized—the body that moved nonchalantly before them was lovely! But there was another reason they were all surprised and silent: the naked body that everyone, myself included, found so attractive, so deeply moving belonged to a six-year-old little girl. Each of us wondered the same thing: "What is this stranger doing here, in this space reserved for men? Is the women's hamam broken or what?"

The little girl didn't bother herself with the curious and hungry looks that longed to unravel the mystery of her. She looked for a spot and found one in the middle room, between the hottest room where the basin is enthroned and the coldest. She sat, waiting for her father to fill the buckets with water.

Naturally, as though she had always washed her lovely body in our old hamam, she began the rites, letting her father, who was completely unaware of the way he was turning the place upside down, take care of her from time to time. It seemed she was a pervert: not content to pose in ways that let everyone see (the light had been lit in the meantime) into her depths, she shamelessly looked at the men who surrounded her, unembarrassed, staring at each in turn. And even as some of them busied themselves washing their private parts, that just made her bolder, anxious to know what was hiding in their underwear, undoubtedly wondering why they didn't take them off as she had done. In her head we were all uptight, too self-conscious.

A few moments later, her father joined his little Eve in her preferred mode of dress.

The vision of those two in the hamam was surely worth the six-dirham entry fee; if the owner had known what was happening inside, he would have raised the price. Lucky for us, he was absent as usual—the women's hamam next door, with its eternal renovations, took up all his time.

I generally never spent more than an hour at the hamam, since I can only stand so much suffocating heat. That day, I stayed for three: I didn't want to miss a thing, what they gave us was so exceptional, especially since it wouldn't happen again anytime soon. I even forgot to wash myself.

I watched and watched. And suddenly, I found myself in a different hamam, full to the brim, too noisy—in another body, small, too small. I pretended to cling to my mother and sister, half naked. I too had gone to a different hamam than the one that was originally meant for me. How could I, a boy who would someday be a hairy man, have entered this harem without eunuchs, found my place there, and shocked nobody?

This was how I came to understand that women were much more tolerant than men, much freer. I got the message and, as I left the hamam that night, unwashed (I would have had to pay six more dirhams to be honest), I smiled at the little six-year-old girl, with her naked and lovely body, murmuring "Thanks" under my breath.

13.

In Search of Paul Bowles

A friend of mine once declared Paul Bowles "the greatest living Moroccan writer." He was right. The great writer of Tangier died two days ago, Thursday, November 18, 1999. Now, my dream of meeting him, so often postponed, is lost forever. I will never be able to see him. I have to stop dreaming of him, of myself before him.

There are people who accompany us through life from a distance, through their wit, through their works. Paul Bowles is one of these people for me. As long as writers have held an important place in my daily life, Bowles has been haunting me. As I always do when I fall in love with a writer's work, I didn't read all of him, all at once. I wanted to make it last. Even more: without meaning to, I created a Paul Bowles fan club all around me. The day my friend Saadia saw me reading *A Distant Episode* in the garden of the Mohammed V University in Rabat, she asked, "Who's this Malika you're reading about?" So I told her the magnificent story of "Here to Learn," a novella about a young girl from a village in the Rif Mountains who somehow manages to become part of the super-exclusive jet set without really wanting to, with the help of a Spanish photographer. Saadia stopped me in the middle of my account: she'd already decided that she was going to read the book as soon as I was done. A month later, our whole class knew Malika's story. The desire for more pushed all my classmates to read other books by Paul Bowles, and not just his short stories. That's why there was such a long waiting list to borrow his books from the library at the French Cultural Institute of Rabat.

I've visited Tangier twice. The first time, I was ten and knew only one writer, Mohamed Choukri, but at the time I didn't know he lived in Tangier. Nor did I know that *For Bread Alone* had first been translated into English by Paul Bowles, before Tahar Ben Jelloun translated it into French. I was twenty-two years old when I set foot in Tangier again. By then, I'd received my *licence* in French literature and I was familiar with the author of *The Sheltering Sky*. It was in hopes of meeting him, among others, that I'd gone to that mythic city with my Swiss friend, Guy. Before going, I'd read Daniel Rondeau's *Tangier*, in which he dedicates an entire chapter to Bowles and his wife Jane and even practically gives away their address and Paul's schedule. This is how I knew that every day around two in the afternoon Bowles went to pick up his mail at the post office on Boulevard Mohammed V or Victor Hugo and often proceeded to the Haffa Café. With this information, I didn't doubt for a moment that I'd be able to meet him. In the worst case, I'd ask Mme Rachel, the owner of the no less famous Les Colonnes bookstore, to give me his exact address, not his phone number. (He'd always refused to install a phone, being partial to epistolary exchanges.) I had twelve days in that city that was falling into ruin before your very eyes. Plenty of time.

Tangier is a possessed city, haunted by spirits of different faiths. When we have literature in our blood, in our souls, it's impossible not to be visited by them. To stay in Tangier is to succumb to the charm of these spirits. They're everywhere. And if every once in a while we are surprised to find ourselves eating more than we need to, it's because they are in us. We see the city with their eyes. We love it for them. They live because of us.

This same welcome awaited Henri Matisse on his first trip to Tangier, a trip that would have deep and long-lasting effects on his painting: it rained the whole time, all twelve days I was there. I wasn't too discouraged. Up to the very end, I waited for Paul Bowles to emerge from around a street corner. I waited for fortune, which does and undoes everything, to smile upon me. Never. He'd obviously become more of a homebody than ever. Given the constant rain, this seemed plausible.

My trip ended before I had the chance to meet him. I left, letting the heavens weep with a vengeance. I was miserable the whole train-ride home. Arriving in Rabat, where the sun shone generously, I saw how wrong I'd been. In fact, I had been with Bowles, I had talked to him and seen him. He was by my side the whole time. We had spoken with each other, shared many stories. He had accompanied me.

I kept this state of mind for as long as I could. Life is never the same once we decide what does or doesn't make us happy. We cling to it. I dove into the rest of his works, he who'd sometimes understood Morocco better than Moroccans, who'd smuggled many gifted artists out of the shadows. Afterwards, I saw the excellent movie Bernardo Bertolucci had made of *The Sheltering Sky* with two great actors, Debra Winger and John Malkovich. It's easy to forget that at the very beginning of the film Bowles appears, seated at a café table in the Grand Socco, elegantly dressed, with an intelligent gaze that travels beyond the visible. He is the storyteller. We meet him again at the end. Port is dead. Kit returns to Tangier, the starting point. She sees our writer; they give each other a long look. Unforgettable.

Not long after, two of my friends will actually meet him. In Tangier of course, which he never leaves. The first, Philippe, the Swiss German, will speak with him for an hour at the Haffa café— "one of the most wonderful moments of my life," he told me later. The second, René de Ceccatty, will land a wonderful interview with him that will be published in *Le Monde*. I had not yet met René when I read it. He will speak proudly of Bowles from our very first meeting. He'll tell me about his emotions, his impressions.

I was satisfied, if a bit jealous. And still, despite everything: the dream that someday luck would be on my side and I'd be given the same treatment as my friends. I prepared myself for this meeting. What questions would I ask, what would I tell him about myself, about my life? And most importantly, I was prepared to watch and listen closely. Learn, continue to learn. It's true, I could have contented myself with his books, they're rich enough. But when we catch the literary bug, we become insatiable, we always want more.

Paul Bowles, the Moroccan writer, is dead. When I heard the news, I looked for my copy of the CD of Moroccan music he recorded a long time ago. I couldn't find it, I'd loaned it to a friend. But this music, his music, lives in my head. No need for a CD.

14.

Starobinski's Baraka

Who was it that first introduced me to the great Swiss writer Jean Starobinski? It must have been one of my professors at the University of Rabat.

Like Roland Barthes, Philippe Lejeune, Gaston Bachelard and many others, Jean Starobinski was one of those writers, those intellectuals quoted frequently in university courses. They benefited from a certain aura; you could sense their importance, their grandeur when people talked about them. Those who knew their work were fortunate, luckier still those who managed to understand their thought—it was not always easy. During exams, we absolutely had to mention them in our essays and written commentaries to show that we were well read, curious. Using their proposals judiciously was a demonstration of one's intelligence and would earn a considerably higher grade. We would do whatever it took to get good grades, even memorize quotes—I've done it so many times. I don't know what it was that so fascinated me about Jean Starobinski throughout my first two degrees. His name must have been for something in that fascination, a name at once mysterious and clear, musical and difficult to pronounce—at least in the beginning. Later, we would refer to him simply as Staro (we could do that; he was a friend). I sometimes quoted him in the epigraphs to my papers. I was proud to know him. I was satisfied by my studies: my only joy.

We do not merely live with the people who surround us physically, we also live in the company of spirits—those we admire, those we adore, their sensibilities, their ways of looking at things. We evolve with them, thanks to them.

They accompany us.

Time passes.

Fortune smiled upon me. I was sent to finish my studies in Switzerland, in Geneva, Jean Starobinski's city. He had retired, but still frequented the halls of the university. He was always available. You could feel that he still had more to give, to pass on, to impart.

A friend of mine who was a professor at that university introduced me to him. The feeling when he touched my hand (I didn't wash it for the rest of the day), when he took interest in me, was unforgettable. That's his great power: his curiosity. He wanted to know me, to be kept apprised of my studies (which focused on the 18th century, his specialty, his century). One week later, at my request, we made an appointment to meet in his office. I had an appointment, not just with a man, but with ideas and thoughts embodied precisely by that man whose gaze was so frank and direct. With a school of criticism, the Geneva school,

I thought about my friends in Morocco, about how jealous they would be, and how wonderful I'd feel when I told them the news, how I'd savor that feeling. There had to be more to talk about than the simple, trivial fact of the meeting. Things were going to happen. I would need to remember them, provoke them, actively participate in this exchange with Starobinski, even if I did so in complete silence.

In Morocco, when a person is successful, we touch our clothing to theirs so that we might have a bit of their success, a bit of their baraka. At the university, when the results of written exams are announced each May, these scenes play out again and again: students who've passed their exams let themselves be touched by those who've failed. In this way, the latter would glean extra luck (and thus, baraka) for the next exams. All students, boys and girls alike, participate in this ritual. Some even try to get a little something more out of it, forgetting that such actions risk compromising the transmission of the baraka.

Before my meeting with Starobinski, I set a goal for myself. I was going to touch his clothing. In light of all his accumulated successes, he surely had a deep well filled with baraka. I needed just a bit of it, this non-Muslim, Jewish baraka, which was above all an intellectual, literary baraka. Starobinski had suddenly become a saint to me; an honored saint, a saint to honor.

Of course I showed up for our meeting very early. Of course I was afraid. My heart beat quickly and irregularly. But oddly enough, I didn't feel small. In Morocco, in front of certain important people—usually rich people who were full of disdain for those of lower social standing—I suffered a horrible inferiority complex. None of that in front of this great man, this "alim" as we would say where I come from. He put me at ease right away by asking me almost banal questions about my daily life. Had I found a place to live? Where? Was my scholarship adequate? Did I already miss Morocco? He told me a bit about himself, his projects, his travels. He even gave me a gift: an article related to my thesis that he'd annotated himself. This gift alone was an incredible baraka, a written record of Starobinski's thought process, a light. I was crazy with joy: yes, but you mustn't give up on your goal. You absolutely must touch his clothing. Don't be afraid. You need to see this through. Don't you realize how lucky you are?

Seated face to face with Starobinski, as he spoke to me slowly about serious matters, as he looked me straight in the eyes, as he made recommendations that I jotted down in my notebook and gave me guidance for my research, I had no idea how I would reach my goal, which suddenly seemed harebrained, absurd. Nonetheless, deep within me, a voice insisted. It wouldn't leave me alone.

So I'd shown up with two missions. The first was carried out marvelously. I learned so much when I was with Starobinski (the Master). The second, however, made things difficult for me. I tried to sweep it from my mind by asking questions. In vain. Two hours later, that voice was still hounding me.

Starobinski came to my rescue. He offered to take me on a tour of the department's well-stocked library. He stood up. I did the same. I hurried to the door, opened it, and waited for him to pass. That's when the "miracle" happened. He picked up a copy of Rousseau's *Confessions* from his desk and came over to me to share a passage. He was very close to me. We were touching. I was touching his clothing just as I'd hoped. For a long time. Rapture.

Did Starobinski's baraka really transfer over to me? Only time will tell. While I wait, the memory of this meeting helps me survive, pushes me forward on my little path.

M'Barka must be proud of me.

15.

I'd Like to Be a Book

As soon as I got to Paris, I started watching people, observing them. The French, Parisians. Faces, bodies, silhouettes, clothing, I followed them with my eyes and never had my fill. People everywhere say that Paris is where it's at. And I was there, where it's at. My God, were there things to see! I looked on, hungrily. I looked, especially in the metro; everywhere else, Parisians ran, they didn't even have a second to look at me. Because they didn't. They were thinking about dinner, the supermarket that closes at 7:30, the 8 o' clock news, the concert at 8:30, gotta hurry, there's no time. They run and run, even on weekends. Oh, the weekend. They think about it from the very first day of the week. And vacation? That word is always on everyone's lips, it's the main topic of discussion among Parisians.

Parisians had no time to look at me. I rushed to the FNAC store at Les Halles the very first week of my trip and there, I waited desperately in hopes that I'd catch someone's eye, just one eye, even half of one. Nothing. I didn't exist. I was an invisible man. I saw them, examined them, studied them like a painter studies his models, I honored them. And me? I was alone. I went from person to person, over and over. Alone.

In Morocco, it would never have been like that. Luckily. In Morocco, when you leave home, you must make sure you're dressed well, or at least decently. Passersby stare at you shamelessly, inconsiderately. The girls are the true specialists in this art: observing and criticizing others. Searching for the flaw. Looking, only looking at the surface. And passing judgment based on these impressions. Many people are fine with this, they see no need to work at understanding. At the University of Rabat, I had a colleague who did that—she was simultaneously abhorrent and fascinating. Because she was friends with my best friend, the sweet and energetic Saâdia, I'd occasionally find myself spending time with or around her. Her name was Souad, a lovely name that didn't fit her at all. It implied a sort of refinement, which she had none of, even though her mother originally came from Fes, the city where refinement verges on absurdity, madness. She apparently hadn't inherited any of these manners. When I saw Souad, all of a sudden a mean saying would pop into my head: "Neither pretty nor punctual." And it's true, she wasn't pretty, too tall, too brown, always dressed in her inevitable black jeans: Levi's, she'd make sure to specify. Dressed like that— and she only wore espadrilles—she looked like a tomboy. I never liked her, she annoyed me. But at the same time, I was fascinated with her. Her words exasperated me to no end and I listened, despite myself: "Look at this one! Where did she learn to mix colors like that? Mallow green with egg yolk yellow! It's nauseating. If I was her, I wouldn't leave the house, I'd save myself and everyone else the embarrassment. It's indecent. And her hair! Shameful, she looks like a kindergartener. I mean really, there are limits. Not everyone can be a mdiniyya. If you come from the country, you should at least make an effort, learn, there are rules."

One day, she caught sight of a very tall man from a distance. All at once, her tongue loosened—poor guy! If he'd only heard what she was saying about him: "Look at that walking ladder, he must be a house painter, I can't see any other job he could do. Look, look, his pants are way too small for him. Of course no size exists to fit that body, but my God, go to a tailor! Really, some people… Who do you think will ever marry him? Where will he find a woman his size? There aren't many tall women in this city. Ha! Imagine them in bed, his lady and him, naturally small and way too tall. What a tragedy. How will they manage? It's too complicated."

She could go on forever, with her vivid imagination. That's the part of her personality I found so fascinating, how her fertile imagination made up stories at full speed… mean stories that would crack us up, Saâdia and me, until our stomachs and jaws ached. Souad remained unruffled—she was serious, serious about badmouthing people. She was always ready for it. She was like a witch who is not afraid of djinns or of the devil. She even practiced her favorite sport in class, because you see, most of our professors were women. It goes without saying that she preferred them to the men, who she disregarded entirely—she'd only attack them if she had absolutely no other material or subjects.

I dispised her, but that doesn't mean she didn't leave her mark on me. How do we forget the mean girls? Impossible, we never forget bad criticism, bad grades, bad memories. I dispised her, I didn't know how to defend myself from her attacks. I was unfamiliar with the linguistic register she used. She attacked me with words full of insinuation, words that hurt bad, bad, women's words. She'd berate me for my lack of personality (what did she know about it?), my weakness around certain girls who I really liked but she hated (jealous!). She'd rehash certain scenes and then tell me that I should have reacted (I had to be a man, like her boyfriend. But what does it mean to be a man? I still don't know). She judged my life, my clothing of course, my haircut, everything. She couldn't stop herself, she kept trying to show me what to do and what not to do, always acting high and mighty, superior. As if to say: "I'm a reference, never forget it."

I stopped seeing her. I avoided her. Coward that I was, I couldn't manage to give it to her straight, tell her what I thought about her. She never went out without an entourage—she needed an audience for her performances. I dispised her and it was reciprocal: she had no respect for me, I have no doubt she saw me as a different kind of creature, certainly not a man. Souad was the only girl who scared me. One day, she'd become a novelist, a writer of romance novels.

In rummaging through my past, my childhood, I've found others like Souad. When I was little, my mother would bring me with her to weddings. At these events, all women were queens, rivals in beauty (who would be the fairest of them all?), dressed in caftans or takchitas, eyes lined with kohl, pink cheeks, lips turned orange by the miswak, their hair beautifully styled and without scarves, covered in too much perfume. During these ceremonies, at first glance, it all seemed harmonious, the understanding true, the happiness complete: but the truth was very different. Women were torn between two positions, they faced a real dilemma, they were filled with fire. On the one hand, they were dying to show off their jewels, their prettiest outfits, make it known that, *everything is perfect at home, my husband spoils me, he buys me everything I want, look at all my gold jewelry...* They absolutely had to let everyone know and, most of all, news had to spread. All the women had this aim well in sight, and they used all their resources to get there. But on the other hand, they were afraid of attracting the evil eye. Showing off is a sure way to attract evil eyes, which will do everything in their power to reach the desired end. How many times had my mother turned down invitations just so she could be left alone! How many times, when she found out that our neighbor El-Kamela would be at a party, did she send me to apologize to the celebrating family for her, saying that she was sick and couldn't even move!

Wedding parties are paradise to women like Souad and El-Kamela. The latter was even more ruthless. Her eye caught and criticized everything and everyone. (People said she actually was a witch.) Everyone made especially sure that children did not pass under her malevolent gaze.

The days after these parties are even worse. Women in the neighborhood would meet in groups of three and four to check the score sheet. These meetings had many harmful repercussions. They broke up families, destroyed couples, shattered still fragile happiness.

In Morocco, nobody is ever left alone, privacy is nonexistent. You have to fight to earn it, and I fought. You're followed everywhere you go. You're never alone. There's no solitude where I come from. Old people, even when they're sick, paralyzed, are never alone. I adapted to this system, it was with me even when I rebelled against it. This way of life will always be with me, in a string of images. They follow me everywhere. When I got to Paris, I was surprised to find that I harbored a kind of affection for this system. I didn't want to admit it to myself, but I missed it. There's nothing more frightening than indifference, the sense of non-existence, of death. I realized that, like everyone else who comes from my country, I was curious about people, hungry for them. I was in need of stories. Moroccan stories.

I walked around Paris within a general state of indifference. It was during this time that I wished to be a book, printed in thousands of copies. A book I could hand out to every Parisian. That way, they would have to read me, to look at me. This book would have no title.

16.

A Life Elsewhere, or the Translator

When I first arrived in Europe, everything seemed new to me. Even though I had spent many years studying the civilization of this Western world. I had the culture, I believed I knew it perfectly. Yet, there is a great difference between studying something and living it. From a distance, Europe looked like paradise to me. That is not all it is. Living there is something else entirely. I appreciated tremendously being able to say: "Today I want to visit Titian's 'Man with a Glove' at the Louvre, to say hello, to remind him that I have not forgotten him." This is a rare liberty. One must recognize the luck that accompanies it, never forget it.

Strangely, by being close to the object of my studies, my mind, which may have had its fill, began to force this upon me: constant thoughts of Morocco. Morocco came back to me, called upon me forever. It followed me each time I moved. As such, each time I encountered this object, a reflection gradually began developing in my mind, almost unbeknownst to me, concerning my country of origin. I became and continue to be fascinated about this duality. It occasionally provokes in me a strange feeling that is difficult to describe: I lose all my bearings and am lost, unstable in large European cities. They call this state depression. Me, depressed! I'm not so sure about that... I would say instead that I live in between:

each of the two cultures pulls me to its side (so there is a battle in me, in my body). This can be enriching—and it is—but also deeply destabilizing. Already, in Morocco, there were days when I was unwell. Here, with no spiritual protection but the prayers of my mother back home, it's even worse when things are bad.

The worst, Malika lived it when she left for Geneva in the mid-1980s. I was twelve years old, I had just run away for the first and only time.

Malika. I never met her and yet I know her whole life story. One day in Geneva, during the summer of 1998, I was hired by a shifty Swiss German to orally translate into French fifty or so letters written in Arabic. The man inspired a great uneasiness in me from the moment I met him and I immediately regretted having answered his ad. I thought the worst: he seemed like a secret agent of the Mossad. There was nothing to confirm this suspicion. Nothing to disprove it either... I was afraid. Luckily what I discovered in the letters was rich and intriguing. My whole life. Malika's life.

The letters all had the same subject: Malika. She'd written the first ones. (How did this Swiss German, who never even gave me his name, come to have these letters that were sent to Morocco? Mysterious.) She wrote that she was well, that she had been very kindly welcomed by her aunt's friend. She was trying to sort out her situation. She had yet to find work but her aunt's friend wanted to bring her into the home of some very good nassara, Christians: she had spoken with them about it and all would be worked out soon. She never complained, she only said that she missed the village (Gharb, near Kenitra) from time to time. The weather was good to her: "It is very hot, a different heat from ours, dry. In the streets, everyone is naked. They like the color of my skin and they like my hair too, which I never dared show in our dear country because it is thick, too frizzy." Her comments were not extensive: one got the feeling that she was suddenly becoming aware of her beauty, of her body. She was happy about it. Later, that body would become a weapon.

The Moroccan responses to her letters were there too, they came regularly and almost exclusively from women. Women who didn't know how to write and who most often hired a public writer. They all wished her good luck, prayed for her and for her future, which would surely be glorious because she was now far away from the "crisis," from the "qahra." They all requested one thing of her: that she not forget them.

The letters that came from Morocco all began the same way. They invoked God, the prophet Mohammed, the apostles, and the saints, in long paragraphs that seemed like they would never end. Then they paused and they wrote "and after this…" Finally, they seemed to be getting to the heart of the matter, but no, not at all, they launched into greetings: citing all of the names of family members, young and old, friends, neighbors. When someone left Morocco, suddenly they became more important, they were considered lucky, mabrouk. So Malika was mabrouka: she was going to make money. It was important that she not forget them, they had to write to her, to remind her that she had left us alone, that without her we were nothing, that her place was empty, that we missed her… The sentiments were true. Not always. The prayers were sincere if self-serving, because you must understand that the people who stay behind imagine that in Europe money falls from the sky, tumbling through the clouds that hide the sun for most of the year.

Malika quickly became "rich," which is to say that she had enough money to send gifts to everyone regularly. The land of chocolate and watches continued to warmly welcome her, even if the cold had come at last and the sunlight had drawn away, then disappeared.

In the beginning, she found work as a nanny with her aunt's friend's nassara. They were very nice and they regularly offered her clothes, so much clothing in fact that she sent much of it to Morocco. They are the ones who helped her get her papers. She was grateful to them. She constantly thanked them in her letters. Two years later, she had a house, and her name was Malika Barras. She had married a Swiss man. I imagined her family's reaction. No letter mentioned it. They were obviously scandalized, but how could they express it or protest? She was so far away, out of their grasp, even the men could do nothing. She had made a life for herself and her family, she was free. In Morocco, a woman can easily gain her freedom when she makes money. To put it simply, she buys herself.

Malika was still a good Muslim. I learned from one sentence that her husband was named Kamal, so he must have converted to Islam. There was no problem, even if this conversion was merely an administrative move necessary to silence her family, who now assessed that her honor was intact, despite knowing the truth…

Then, the tone of the letters changed. It's not that they forgot their prayers (quite the opposite, they were even more long-winded on the subject), but they began to demand of Malika the things that they had really wanted for a long time but had dared not request: shoes with rubber soles for her aunt's son; coats for all, young and old, since winter had become more and more difficult to endure in Morocco; fabric for both of her father's wives (they wanted to make caftans, it would soon be summer, the season filled with weddings and other happy events; they had to prepare ahead of time); pens, notebooks, medication, designer perfumes and of course Swatch watches and chocolate. She fully satisfied each of these wishes, she had no choice. Later, they would send her photocopies of bills to pay (rent, electricity, taxes) to prove to her that their requests for money were real and also, without a doubt, to lay the fait accompli before her: if you don't save us, we will be ruined, you are our only hope, we have nobody else to ask, you are our light, our angel... If Malika had refused they would have considered her a traitor, maybe even a snob, and quickly forgotten what she had done for them up to that point. Malika had agreed to sacrifice herself for others, she did not work for herself but for her whole family, for the Eid lamb, for her uncle's eye operation, for her cousins' school supplies, and even to pay the psychic that her aunt Zohra regularly visited. (Her husband beat her, drank too much, and didn't contribute a single dime to the household. It had to be taken care of, nothing of his manhood should remain but his name—this mission would be an overwhelming success for her.)

Malika had not yet learned to say no, but it would not be long until she did. In the early nineties, she realized that this completely exploitative situation could not last. She became sly, like all of her fellow countrymen: from that point forward, she considered all the money she sent to her family to be a loan, except when it came to her parents, her brothers, and her sisters. In this way, she managed to find a bit of momentary peace.

In 1992, she returned to Morocco for the first time, accompanied only by her daughter Sarah. It was a celebration, everyone showed her how much they loved her, reminded her how important she was to the family. She was now the head of the family, more a man than the men. Strangely, nobody took the time to ask her about her work (what was it that she did exactly?), and she never spoke of it. The essential thing was that she had money. Money resolved everything, it could even turn a "maskhout" into a "mardhi." Her whole family blessed Malika, they prayed for her even more.

During this trip, she decided to have a house built in Kenitra. Her father wanted it closer to him, in the village, and he told her so, but his opinion no longer mattered as it once had. So Malika said she would send him to Mecca to wash himself of all his sins. He kissed her on the head. She had her house built the way she wanted it, where she wanted it.

This trip was marred by an incident that disturbed the "peace" in which everyone lived. (They lacked for nothing, they could buy anything.) Habiba, Malika's cousin and her best friend before she left, did not come to greet her, not the first day nor the second nor any other. The message was as clear as could be: Habiba was jealous, she still lived with her parents, did the cleaning each day, cooked, washed, tidied up, made everything neat. She and Malika were the same age, 32, and she still wasn't married, despite her great beauty. Malika did not talk about it in her letters, but Habiba must have held her responsible for everything that happened to her. She had taken all the luck; she had gone to live freely somewhere else, far from constraints and machismo. She had left her, abandoned her. Habiba could not forgive her. She would have her revenge.

That's where the worst began; from there, it would swell and swell…

Malika returned to Geneva happy, full of energy, as brown as she had once been, but with a slight pain she couldn't define. She spoke of it in the first letter she wrote to her family. Nothing serious. She still wanted to build a house in Morocco and gave very precise instructions.

With time, the letters came from her less and less frequently, barely twenty in six years. Still, this was enough to follow the evolution of her pain. She was sick. She never specified with what. Her family continued to inundate her with missives, they prayed even more for her, they wondered what exactly she had: she didn't respond. She felt bad. Her aunt Zohra who consulted psychics wanted to come see her. "Perhaps someone cast a spell on you when you came to Morocco. A jealous person, Morocco is full of those. Let me come see you. I'll be able to locate your pain. Or you could come back here, we'd call upon the saints…" Malika did as she pleased. She stayed in Switzerland.

I got to the end of the story: only two letters were left to read. The first was a sort of will: Malika left everything that she had to her daughter Sarah, who she delivered into her aunt's care. The second, a document from a Swiss office, spoke of the repatriation of Malika's body. She had died. Of what? No answer.

I looked up at the Swiss German, who listened to me religiously. I don't know where I found the courage to ask him: "What did Malika do for work?" He answered me right away, tersely: "High-class prostitute."

He paid me 120 Swiss francs for five hours of work. I was very pleased. I was very unhappy. And my head was filled with questions.

17.

The King Is Dead

I am in Paris. And the king, our king Hassan II, the only king I have ever known, has just died. He really died.

I was returning home from the movies, happy to have watched Quentin Tarantino's *Pulp Fiction* again at L'Arlequin, on the Rue de Rennes. Three messages were waiting for me on the answering machine. They all told me the same terrible news, an EVENT: the king is dead! Hassan II is deceased.

A chill down my spine. Incredulity. The impossibility of such a thing. He has left this life! He has left this life! At first, the sheer enormity of the news would not allow me to confront it, to truly believe it. As though I hadn't heard it. What are they saying to me, what are they trying to tell me? I listened to the three messages a second time, then a third, then a fourth. I had trouble finding meaning in the words, finding the corresponding words in Moroccan Arabic. The messages were real, sure, my three friends' voices trembled as though they couldn't believe it either. They were calling me to check whether I had also heard the tragic news. They wanted to know how I was feeling at that specific moment. But I was unable to experience emotion. I was shocked.

I stayed like that for a long time, staring at the ceiling, dazed, paralyzed, trying in vain to understand that Hassan II was dead, dead… Which is to say, no longer of this world.

A little later, turbulent images would come to me, descend upon me, rise up before and behind my eyes with no discernible order, images at once precise and fleeting.

I feel tempted to arrange them, organize them, in my search for their original meaning.

Which would be the first? What is the first memory I have of the king?

This question was answered with the sudden arrival of an image of the lamb festival, Eid El-Kebir. My father always wanted to wait until after the king slaughtered his lamb to slaughter ours. He'd say: "Hassan II is our guide, our imam. He inherited the title of Commander of the Faithful from his father Mohammed V. It is clear, he is the Commander and we must follow him, wait… And as you know, he is one of the descendants of the prophet Mohammed, peace and prayers be upon Him. If we slaughter our lamb before his, not only is it a sign of disrespect, but our sacrifice will have no value before God. We will only have meat, with no blessing, no spirituality. We have no choice. We wait. We will eat eventually. The lamb is not going to run away." When he wanted to, my father could be very convincing: it was like a religious lecture, with quotes from the Koran and even from the Hadith. We kept our mouths shut. We had to wait. Hassan II first and foremost.

The problem is that the king never slaughtered his lamb before noon, during which time he performed the Eid prayer and received endless compliments from the kingdom's highest dignitaries and ambassadors. Like us, the other sheep waited, waited and, feeling the approach of death, bleated nervously; they called to each other from one end of the city to the other. They were saying goodbye.

This was a fearsome, unbearable spectacle, which made us even more determined to complete this normally happy ritual as quickly as possible. Of course, some neighbors did not share our patience and by 10 in the morning they had carried out their religious sacrifices. At 11 o'clock, they were already grilling. Imprisoned in the silence of the wait, we envied them even as we felt sorry for them. When at last we had in our hands those delicious skewers covered in cumin, which we ate with a very special pleasure, all was forgotten. We were truly content. And the pleasure was all the more intensified by the fact that we had waited such a long time.

Another memory, of another kind. Although… I was still in elementary school— in the early eighties. Thousands of young men and women had taken to the streets to protest, to give voice to their hunger. The price of bread, they later told me, had gone up. People did whatever they could to eat, to survive, and sometimes they even stole. But in Morocco, the big criminals had left nothing behind, they'd taken it all. They didn't pay for bread; it was given to them. I was hungry too, incidentally, growing hungrier and hungrier. My father, whose salary was less than 1,500 dirhams, had a lot of trouble making ends meet and at the end of each month he fell even deeper into debt. We were always living on credit (with the vegetable vendor, with the butcher, with the repairman). The young people shouting in our place had been mistreated. With my own eyes, I'd seen the police beating them, shooting at them. The young people had fled screaming ever harder, some of them had fallen down and never gotten back up (their bodies disappeared too, their families would never get to bury them with dignity). Images like these can never be forgotten. Already, in my child's mind, two essential questions persisted: who was responsible for this massacre of which we were forbidden to speak, even in private? Who gave the orders that would keep us ignorant and poor?

We saw Hassan II every day, his portraits were everywhere, he followed us wherever we went. On television, they talked about him daily, his interviews, his visits, everything (absolutely everything!) he did. We had been taught to love looking at him, to rejoice in all of his actions, and even to appreciate his elegance, his varied and numerous outfits, traditional and modern. He certainly did have taste. So we truly, sincerely loved looking at him, and he gave us many occasions to do so. When he went to greet his guests at the Salé airport, his cortege would drive past my school: of course, on those days we didn't have class on the sole condition that we go cheer him on as he passed by: "Long live the king! Long live Hassan II!" So I saw him many times in his superb car, waving his hands to greet the crowds that shouted his name and prayed for him. He was far away from us. He went by very quickly.

Such a presence leaves its mark on the mind, the subconscious, and contributes greatly to myth. The myth of Hassan II focused on his baraka. Everyone in Morocco knew that he had always been incredibly lucky. He was protected, they said, by certain spirits.

At the end of each school year, Hassan II would gather the best students in the kingdom at his palace. As a child, I had long harbored the dream of becoming one of those students. The dream of approaching him and, inevitably, kissing his hand like my own father's. To do that, I would have to become the best student, not only in my school, but in the whole city of Salé. My dream remained a dream.

It was my oldest brother, Abdelkebir, who would make it come true in my place. After working at the Ministry of the Interior for ten years, one fine day he was appointed by royal decree to a high position. This afforded him the privilege of being received by the king and, consequently, of kissing his hand several times. This crucial moment was immortalized in a photo that still hangs in Abdelkebir's sitting room. I was proud of my big brother, of course, and not at all jealous. It was a significant event in my family, we'd even seen Abdelkebir on the evening news.

Hassan II was like a father to us. In Morocco, the father has extraordinary power over his children. You are expected to accept everything from him, the good and the bad. When he dies, it tears you apart, you mourn him sincerely. Tomorrow, Sunday, all of Morocco will mourn its king, its father, and bid him a memorable and intensely emotional farewell. Tomorrow, all of Morocco will be in Rabat. Tomorrow, all Moroccans, like me, will go over their numerous (and contradictory) memories with this king.

Hassan II died yesterday, Friday, the Muslim holy day. Tomorrow is another day.

18.

The Only Mirror

It was the only mirror we had at home. It belonged to my father, who had bought it at the flea market and framed it like a painting but did not hang it in the bathroom. Everyone used it: my father and Abdelkebir to shave, my mother and sisters for makeup. And me to admire myself.

Nobody in my family, nobody around me, told me that I was handsome: even when one isn't, one sometimes wants to hear it. None of them would comment on my physique, on my physical presence. I had become familiar with the feeling of not having a body, though it didn't suit me. The girls in middle school liked me a lot but I didn't see any desire in their eyes for me, for my still-developing body, invaded by adolescent sensations that were new, persistent, irritating because they never led anywhere.

I'd come to this tragic conclusion: I have no body. I only exist in the world as my shadow. Thus, I am black. Not like black Africans, who symbolized to me the very epitome of beauty and finery.

As an insecure but rational teenager, I wasn't always able to face this reality. I would be absent, I would forget myself, stop thinking about myself. I would purposefully let myself go by putting on horrible clothing in gaudy colors that never went together (yellow with orange, green with white and red) and, in the words of my mother, who did not like my look, I let an impenetrable forest grow atop my head. I got my revenge on the whole world and myself: but why isn't my body attractive? am I truly ugly? This is the image I am given of myself; this is what I understand of all this terrible silence around my body. To please them, I will erase it even further, I will imprison myself, cover myself up, go even further… Kill myself?

This was obviously a cry for help. Nobody heard it.

Although I couldn't see it at first, this attitude toward my body was the best way to approach it, to pay attention to it and its evolution. To look at it. To love it?

From time to time, I would take my father's mirror and shut myself in Abdelkebir's room—at this time, he was already working at the Ministry of Information. He didn't spend as much time at home as he used to, which gave me—and my sisters too—time to penetrate the intimacy of his room and spend brief moments there. I would enter through the window: he always locked his door as though he had things to hide. Abdelkebir's room, his scent, his books, the stereo system, the many cassettes (Jimmy Hendrix, James Brown, Pink Floyd, Fela Kuti, Santana, Um Kulthum), the dirty clothes thrown on the ground (of course I tried them on: my brother on me!), my father's mirror and me. The certainty that I would not be bothered and the sweet, gentle heat that always reigned in this room would instill a certain confidence in me. Thus, I dared to confront my image, and my body, and I would finally give myself to myself. I would be reconciled with Abdellah.

I'd place the mirror on Abdelkebir's narrow bed, in which he and I had slept together many times (long and unforgettable hours, our bodies pressed together and our scents mingling). I'd approach the mirror and discovered myself. A long, thin face: pimples on my forehead and chin (I loved popping them), little annoying hairs in my nose, my right eye slightly different from my left, cheeks hollow and starving. No charm. Yes, I was what they didn't say, ugly, uninteresting. I'd abandon myself to this simultaneously delicious and painful narcissism. I would move slightly further away from the mirror to discover the rest of my body, which I didn't know very well when I began taking these particular retreats. And yes, it was as skinny as street cats; but then no, I was not skinny, I was slim, it was better when it was put that way. My skin: except for the bit that covered my hands, my feet, and my face, I did not know my skin. I took my clothes off to touch it (I would slide my hands over my belly, my chest, my breasts, my neck, my thighs, my ass, my penis), greet it, embrace it, taste it.

First the shirt and undershirt: my ribcage was very pronounced, I could even count the ribs; my muscles were nearly nonexistent; my neck was long with a prominent, hard Adam's apple in the middle. You don't eat enough, my poor Abdellah: it's not my fault. One day, I will be in better shape. My bones in particular fascinated me, I found them lovely to look at: hard, firm, they were mine and I loved them. Then my pants and underpants. My God, I'm naked! What a surprise! Is the naked body beautiful? No, it's not. Is mine? No, again. The ass: nothing special, a bit round. The thighs and legs: I believed that this was the most beautiful part of me, they were covered in little hairs, a lovely lawn over which I would tirelessly run my hand. It was so soft! This repetitive movement would rouse my sex: it would grow longer and longer, but where was it going? Neither small nor large, it had not yet known the pleasure of coming in contact with another body. To tell the truth, it didn't look good in my hand, it was in the mirror that suddenly (with the rest of my body) it became elegant: it was other, lovely, and through it my body became other as well. Metamorphosis. Immediately followed by ejaculation: spurts of sperm on the mirror, with its odor I found unpleasant. And still in the mirror's abyss, my naked body and I, sweating, breathless, happy. Then I would approach the magic mirror and kiss it three times in thanks.

For a period of two or three years, I took these retreats regularly, always following the same ritual. In my father's mirror, I was handsome, truly handsome. Nobody in the world could deny this truth. My truth and my body's. My body is no longer so skinny, but it's not fat either, and it still finds its rightful place in mirrors.

19.

Massaouda and the Snake

Even Massaouda's anger had joy in it. She never stayed angry or sad for very long. She always came back to life, to joy, fairly quickly.

My aunt Massaouda was short. Old. I have always known her that way, old; old and still so young in her mind, in her heart. Her joints always ached. The simple gestures of standing up or sitting were torture for her, and a fairly funny spectacle for us. She would play, exaggerating her pain: "Ow, ow, Sidi Abdelkader Jillali stay with me. Stay near me, don't leave me alone. Ow, ow, I can't feel my knees… What is this pain? I don't understand what is happening to me. Who is attacking me like this? Who would make me the laughing stock of the family? Who is the woman who is so mean in her heart that she would curse me? I'm just a little old lady, leave me alone, leave me alone or I will get really mad. Ow, ow, Abdelkebir, come help me, come help your poor aunt who can't walk anymore, come my child… God will avenge me and throw into eternal darkness whoever it is who follows me everywhere to cast this pain in my back, on my path, even at my door… God will have his vengeance on her… There is justice in this life, in this world… Abdelkebir, gently, let me lean on you… Ow, ow, what hell! And to think, I was still hoping to dance at your wedding…"

She was like that. Old and bursting with energy. Almost paralyzed and still very active. Above all, she was very chatty, like my mother, deliciously chatty. Inventive in her language, and free. One day, she came to our house around noon. The only things we had to eat were bread, olive oil and mint tea. We were always broke at the end of the month. We were filled with anger, which leapt from our black eyes, passing between all of us and forming a perfect circle, a total unity. Massaouda, penniless herself, had expected a better welcome from us. We were taciturn, lifeless, tragically famished. We were downcast. A bit shaken, Massaouda lifted her djellaba, sat down on a bench and said provocatively, pointing her finger at me: "Abdellah, go call Saïd the fishmonger from the next street over so he can come fuck me. I'm willing to give myself to him for five dirhams, if he wants. For five dirhams, I'll open my legs! In any case, it won't be the first time." Everyone burst out laughing. Her words were so vulgar, so comic coming from her. We laughed for a while. At her words. And especially at what she didn't know: Saïd the fishmonger was a homosexual.

Massaouda and her brother, my father, were very close. Too close. They would often go off to darkened corners of our house to talk in lowered voices about their secrets. They easily confided in each other. They looked like two inseparable cats. Massaouda had a lot of authority over my father: Mohammed always listened to her, attentive, docile. Each time she found the two of them together, my mother made the same ironic comment: "She's charging him like you charge a battery. What does she want? To marry him off again? He doesn't have the means, we already can't make ends meet…" But this didn't stop them from further devoting themselves to this overly intimate relationship. Nobody in our house could know their very precious secrets. Except for my mother, perhaps. But she always stayed quiet on the subject.

Massaouda knew many stories. She carried them within her and developed them over time, expanding on them and nourishing them so that she could offer them to us at night, just before we went to sleep. To this day, I still associate night and sleep with her and her voice: I dream about her, her words, her fabulous, fantastic, all-consuming stories.

Night time is for Massaouda's dreams.

She would sleep with us, the children, among us. She inhabited us and we inhabited her. We'd slip under her skin and she would slip under all of ours. Her gravelly voice, so laden with memories and voyages, was majestic. We would go quiet the instant she began speaking, we were all hers, she could do whatever she wanted with us. Massaouda was only ever good to us. She prepared us for the future, for life. She knew the mistakes we were going to make but didn't try to steer us away from them. She would reveal her own to us, but not all of them. She must have kept some of them to herself, the ones that nobody else would have been able to understand: cherished mistakes, the mistakes she claimed for herself, so often linked to the heart and its business, the heart and its whims, its movements.

Massaouda was a mystery. She never married. Still, she lived her life as she wanted, tasting of all its pleasures, depriving herself of nothing, despite her poverty. She was three colors: blue for her tattoos, red for her hair, and yellow for her clothing. They combined to create her personality. She approached her desires with courage. Free. And this movement seemed natural for her, obvious: nobody was offended by it. Quite the opposite: everyone admired her. She was the only one who knew the truth about my father's birth, who was his real father? Another mystery.

With age, her words became more and more enigmatic, one might have called them philosophical. We didn't always understand what she said. We were completely fascinated and filled with doubt.

Was she crazy? We often asked ourselves this question. She was deeply afraid of death and darkness.

Toward the end, the three final years of her life, she suddenly took to smoking occasionally. The smoking philosopher, this time we were really shocked. All of us. We asked her questions about this sudden mania. She would look at us sadly and not answer. The answer undoubtedly rested in that eloquent silence.

Her style of smoking was clumsy and comical. She would go into the courtyard of our home, hide behind the pots where my father had planted tomatoes and fava beans, and smoke cheap Favorites cigarettes. She smoked slowly, slowly, as though her life depended on this smoke that surrounded her entirely, on the outside and the inside. She disappeared behind it. Each time, she would smoke three cigarettes in a row. This would last about a half hour. A time for her, for her intoxication and her occupiers. She would often talk about them: "My occupiers didn't let me come, they blocked and paralyzed me. They make me do things I shouldn't do, break laws, ignore regulations." Phantom occupiers. They were in Massaouda and seemed to help her live. They may have forced her to smoke: this guess turned out to be false. I told her about it. In response, she teased me affectionately and then fell silent.

The silence of a woman like her carried the weight of the world.

For a long time, I believed that Massaouda would never share this secret, reveal what was hiding under the rock, what slept within her. One day, once we had stopped asking her for an explanation, she gave us one, but indirectly. She told us a story. The story of Batoule.

A widow with no children. Neither old nor young. Alone. She lived in someone else's home, in everyone's home. She would travel from saint to saint, moussem to moussem, and undoubtedly from man to man. Her husband had died in the War of Independence.

Batoule had lived with him for ten years of quiet happiness. Her in-laws detested her for some unknown reason, so she no longer visited them. Her own family was gone: no mother, no father, no brothers or sisters. What others would take for a true misfortune, Batoule saw as destiny. In order to remain faithful to her dead husband, she decided to continue on the path to happiness. Happiness without too many questions. Happiness that refused to count, not hours, not days, not months. She only cared about the seasons: it was cold, and then one day it was hot.

"The world is large," she would say to people who crossed her path. "I will go wherever my feet will take me, I will sleep wherever people will open their doors to me, I will eat what I am offered, I will even accept charity, and I will give myself to whomever looks at me with kindness, does not judge me and, the very next day, will let me leave and won't try to hold me back. I've freed myself from everything. My husband had every right to me; my body and soul were his. He never, ever abused these rights. He was always with me, beside me. Now, he is forever within me. I am as free as the wind. I am the wind. I only pass through."

She passed through. She never stayed very long. After a period of time, she would pass through the same places again, and see some of the same faces. Six years after her husband died, she had become a kind of mystic, a free poet who aligned herself with God and the djinns. A visionary who touched everyone with the words and incantations she herself had invented. She was surrounded by love, love from another time. Perhaps it was the love you heard of when the spring trees began to sing, a love from the time before Islam had come to Arabia.

Of course in order to push her freedom even further, she decided to smoke. This didn't bother anyone, not even the imams with whom she discussed religion and Sufism, with whom she sometimes spent her nights in the mosques. But she had not made this decision for herself. Batoule was only following the orders of the animal that inhabited her, lived in her and had grown along with her. It was a snake that had taken possession of her body during her first experience of love, an experience to which her parents and the whole douar were opposed. She had followed her desire all the way. At the very moment when she gave herself to her stranger, her mother, with the help of the village witch, called upon all the malevolent spirits and begged them to hasten the death of her daughter, who was going to dishonor her. The malevolent spirits, seeing the sincerity of Batoule's love, settled for a punishment. At first the snake didn't harm Batoule. Then, one day when she was in the mausoleum of a Jewish saint, the snake violently manifested its presence by trying to suffocate Batoule. It climbed into her lungs and launched its evil, its venom. Each time the animal awoke, Batoule thought that she was going to die. She went to the hamam, then to the faquihs in search of a cure. But this was all in vain. She didn't even know what was really going on inside of her. It was an old imam who made her aware of the presence of the snake in her body. He advised her to start smoking: cigarettes to kill the snake!

Batoule told this story whenever she was asked why she smoked. Some believed her. Others thought she was crazy. From another world.

According to Massaouda, Batoule still lived in the Tadla region. She knew her very well: each time she went to the tomb of Saint Moulay Brahim, she would pay her a visit and they would swap stories of their lives. Batoule no longer left this saint, her feet could no longer carry her, she had settled permanently. People came to her to get her baraka, to heal, to flee.

Batoule and Massaouda died the same year. They are buried in the same cemetery, side by side.

20.

From Jenih to Genet

Malika, my mother's cousin, had been living in Larache with her five sons for three years. Her husband had disappeared suddenly, five years after they had moved to this city known for its Roman ruins. He must have left to live with a woman younger than Malika, to join bandits in Mamora, or perhaps to return to his first loves on the Algerian side. Malika wasn't looking for him anymore. After only three months, she had accustomed herself to organizing her life differently, without him, far from her in-laws who'd ruined her life back in the village. Her children were young: the oldest had just begun to study French literature at the university. His name was Ali and he was as handsome as a Berber god. The other four were in middle and high school. Malika's sons were not like the people in the village where they'd grown up. They had a natural, refined elegance that was lovely to see and admire, and which gave them a certain authority. Ali most of all. Later, all the doors would open for them, the doors of life and of the dark and starry heavens during the Sacred Night of Ramadan. Malika knew that she could count on them, so why should she concern herself with a drunkard of a husband who'd beaten her night and day and had forbidden her from going outside and breathing the fresh air of life, the forest, and the sea? With no money, her children still in school, she decided to look for a job. She found one quickly: cooking for a French couple in the neighborhood of Larache where people lived in villas. Her employers were quite kind, especially the man, Guillaume, who helped Malika's sons with their studies. He too was captivated by the magnificent Ali each time he saw him.

My mother M'Barka had not seen her cousin in ten years. And it was the first time I'd met this woman, so close yet so distant and discovered Larache. She looked so much like my mother. They had the same pointed nose, the same almond-shaped eyes, the same tattoos on the chin and between the eyebrows. Malika and M'Barka could have been sisters: one merely had to see them hug each other warmly, feverishly to be convinced of it. The long separation had not altered their feelings, their love, at all. They spoke as though they had never left each other, all the stories, the tales, rushing from their mouths continuously, beautifully. The five boys and I listened to them, rapt— Malika luckily did not have a television. They devoured each other with their eyes and in that moment nobody could have separated them, they had so many things to tell each other, to get out. They were communing.

Of course, I liked Ali a lot. I watched him discreetly, sneakily adoring him with my eyes, and in my heart I held a strong desire to be with him, to go out with him for a moment, just him and me for a moment. Malika, as though she had read my thoughts, saved me: "Ali, my dear, the couscous won't be ready before two o'clock. Take Abdellah into town, show him the streets, the souk, guide him… Take him to Jenih's grave." I didn't know that saint: Saint Jenih. Since I was very young, M'barka had taught me to love saints, their tombs and their baraka. I answered with a plea: "Yes, yes, I want to see the city and especially Jenih…" Ali, kindness incarnate, said: "No problem. Come on, Abdellah. It's been a long time since I last visited that grave."

Ali was 19. I was 13. Ali and I in the empty streets of Larache—it was the sacred Moroccan lunch hour. Ali and I, alone. Ali and I on the mythical road filled with baraka. Ali who watched me, attentive, who put his arm on my shoulder. Ali for me. Ali and his French, which increased my admiration for him. Ali was truly magnificent.

Even deserted, I liked Larache. I sensed its hidden life, its secrets, its mysteries. Ali and I walked for almost an hour. All that was left to see was Saint Jenih. On our path toward him, we met a French man—later, I found out that it was Guillaume, the man Malika worked for. Ali spoke to him in that language that already fascinated me but which I didn't yet understand: French. Ali spoke it comfortably, I was proud of him, happy to be in his company at such a time. Their discussion didn't last very long, just five or six minutes. When he left us, the Frenchman shot me a kindly look and ran his right hand through my curly hair: later, I would understand that he'd liked me.

We were just outside of the city, closer to the blue sea, which was calm that day. I searched in vain for a mausoleum, a kouba, but none appeared, just a Christian cemetery, the Spanish cemetery. "This is where Genet's grave is, in this cemetery near the cliff," Ali said, when he got to the gate. He pronounced it Genet, not Jenih, as his mother had: I didn't understand anything. "Is he a Christian saint?" I asked him. "No, no, he's not a saint. He's a very important French writer who is known all over the world. His name isn't Jenih, as my mom says, but Genet. Jean Genet. Say it!" No need to ask me twice, I tried but I butchered the name of this great writer who was completely unknown to me. Ali couldn't stop laughing.

He laughed at my pronunciation, and it didn't bother me at all: I was thrilled to see him happy, thrilled to see and understand his smile.

Genet was the correct pronunciation, but I preferred saying Jenih like Malika. It was more Moroccan that way, closer to me.

Ali told me later that Jenih loved Moroccans, especially one of them: Mohamed Al-Katrani who lived in Larache and who had just died in a car accident. Jenih had insisted that he be buried in Larache, close to him. So I asked: "Was Jenih in love with Al-Katrani?" Shocked at first, after a few moments of silence, Ali looked me in the eyes and said: "Yes, he loved him... he loved him." And that's it. I had the impression that he knew more and that he didn't want to reveal everything to me. "One day, one day you will know the whole story, Abdellah... Now, let's go to his grave."

A Muslim grave in a Christian cemetery! A simple, white grave overlooking Larache and the sea. A grave between two worlds, two planes, two countries. A grave that rises to heaven, that invites contemplation. A moving grave which could very well have been that of a Muslim or Moroccan saint, the first stone in a mausoleum, a place of pilgrimage for lovers, the unhappy, and those who don't know where to go... It was set in a very beautiful place, eternally flooded with vibrant light, the light of angels and of the martyrs of life, perhaps.

Ali advised me to read some verses from the Koran and to pray for the deceased. I followed his advice naturally, without asking too many questions, overcome with emotion. Jenih loved us, so we should pray for him and for his soul. Two or three minutes passed: communion between two worlds, two lives, two lights; an exchange, a gift... Love, in a way. Peace where I didn't expect to find it, eternally in the air. We breathe it in and it changes us.

We'd been at Jenih's grave for a half hour and Ali still didn't want to leave it. We had to go back home to eat Malika's couscous. "Let's stay here a little longer, Abdellah. Don't you like this place? Don't you like the sea, the words, the sunlight? Just a few more minutes…" As he spoke these words, his face changed, his features were fixed with a deep, vivid suffering, a poignant nostalgia that was impossible to move past. His eyes, drowning in tears, were looking at something beyond mine. They must have been fixed on a memory of past moments, dear, still alive in his heart. I approached him, my body brushed against his and my eyes followed his gaze toward the ocean of the invisible. He placed his left hand on the nape of my neck, then on my left shoulder. He held me close and I asked for nothing more than to be held.

"We've been waiting for you a long time. We didn't want to eat the couscous without you. Did you like Larache, Abdellah?"

"Yes, aunt Malika, I liked it a lot."

"And Jenih?"

"Especially Jenih, auntie. I'd love to go back to his tomb sometime. It's such a special place…"

"I see that you too were touched by him, by his light. He was a great writer, you know."

"Yes, Ali, who has read his books, explained that to me."

"Was he Muslim?" my mother, M'Barka, asked.

"No, cousin."

"So he was an infidel…"

"You know very well that religion is not everything in life, M'Barka. Look at me, I've been able to find more good in Christians than in Muslims. Religion isn't everything."

I will never forget this response, which surprised M'Barka completely and must have inspired her to think differently. As we ate couscous that day, we all thought about Jenih. It was his couscous.

I never saw Malika or Ali or the others again. Three years after that visit, Guillaume, the French man, who had divorced his wife, brought them all to Canada where he'd started a new company. It seems that Malika has become rich, a modern woman, and that she never wants to return to Morocco. I never understood this. And Ali? He'd rather stay there too, far away in America. Did he forget Jenih? No, no of course not, I imagine he still vibrates with emotion when his thoughts turn to that writer. Perhaps he still returns discreetly from time to time to visit, to commune with himself over that grave, to remember at the very site of memory… It's possible.

Ali was right, I ended up learning Jenih's whole story. I now know how to write and pronounce his name correctly, even if deep down I remain faithful to Malika and her way of Arabizing it and appropriating this writer by integrating him into her daily reality. Jenih… Sidi Jenih.

Like Ali, I chose French literature, for my studies and my dreams. For six years, I went to Rabat daily, leaving Salé and its madmen on the other side of the Bou Regreg river. I'd take the number 14 bus and always get off at the second to last station, the one that stops right next to the Moulay Abdellah Garden, where Jean Genet liked to take walks when he visited the Moroccan capital (the garden is always filled with boys, especially in the afternoon). I had to walk an extra ten to fifteen minutes to get to Mohammed V University. On my way, I always passed by the Bar Terminus, across the street from the train station, where the servers and prostitutes still remember the little, balding writer-man with soft, questioning eyes: he always sat at the same table by the windows that overlooked

Boulevard Mohammed V. Very close by, not far from the Place de Baghdad, is the building where Roland Barthes lived during the 1972–1973 academic year. The path of the literati. Learning to better understand French and French literature also meant knowing the story of these writers and what brought them all the way to Morocco, to Rabat. Literature and real life are eternally linked for me, one cannot exist without the other. Life without the words of books seems impossible to live.

At the university, I would find another great surprise in the life of Jean Genet. Abdallah, the tightrope walker! The friend, lover, son, companion, gentle and delicate disciple... This boy, who I discovered in his books, immediately entered into my personal mythology, into my heart. In 1964, he too crossed over to the other world, but his story here below is not yet finished. One day, I will write it.

21.

Murder in Fes

He ran through the crowd barefoot, violently shoving people, determined, crazy. He kept running despite cries of rage and insults. He chased his target, his victim. He carried a big knife in his right hand. He was silent, with fiery red eyes. His victim shouted: "Help! Help me! Save me, save my soul! Help! I'm serious! He's going to…" He didn't even have time to finish his sentence.

Throughout the Fes medina, a heavy, complete silence took hold. The end of the world. Even the muezzin dared not utter the call to prayer. Everything was still. People stopped walking, mouths agape, eyes bulging, heads filled with all possibilities. They imagined the very worst but didn't want to believe it. They looked at each other, searching for answers, confirmation, denial. None came. They were all bewildered and afraid. Their nostrils filled with the smell of death, which suddenly overtook the dark, narrow and mysterious passages of the medina. They breathed it in, they recognized but did not want it.

The silence lingered, growing more and more unbearable. It took on a consistency—now it had a sound that entered through their ears and disturbed their minds substantially. Madness reigned. They were all waiting for deliverance, for the end to this end. Nobody moved, nobody dared to make the slightest gesture. Their hearts were filled with fear. Surprisingly, they made no appeals to God, as though they all knew not to bother him when his nap ran beyond the Al-Asr prayer. Man was left to his own devices, abandoned, totally alone. He suddenly understood his true condition on Earth, he had no more illusions. Everything would end. It would all disappear. The only questions left were how, in what way, and when. Right now, answered a voice that everyone could hear. Right now? Surprise and fear were reflected on all of their faces. They asked themselves again: right now?

The silence was suddenly broken. To tell the truth, it hadn't lasted a very long time, a minute, perhaps a little longer. But all the Fassis had experienced it as an eternity, the eternal hour of the Apocalypse, the moment Time stopped, ended. They even heard the trumpets still sounding, despite the voice that had broken the silence. This voice spoke, then shouted: "He killed him! He killed him… He's dead! He's dead!" A whisper of fear crossed the crowd, followed by a long murmur in unison: "There is no other god but Allah and Mohammed is his prophet!" The return to God was unanimous, crushing. They came back to Him, they pulled themselves together, they confronted fear courageously and recited a few prayers.

The voice continued to shout: "He killed him! Come look, he killed him!" A few seconds later, it added, with the same volume and in the same tone: "He stuck a knife in his stomach. Oh my God! His intestines are coming out of his side…" It strove for accuracy like a television announcer, but it could not control itself, hide its emotion, the horror that the murder scene inspired. The crowd, ever more pious, returned to its prayers for safety.

A murder, here. A crime mere feet from where I was standing.

Who was the murderer and who the victim?

I was afraid too and called out for God's help.

I had just arrived in Fes with two French friends. I was rediscovering this holy, magical, timeless city. I had set a few goals for myself: I would go to the Al-Quaraouine mosque, visit the tomb of Saint Moulay Driss, the son of another saint, Moulay Driss Zerhoun (founder of the city of Fes), buy Fassi henna for my mother, which was as famous all over Morocco as the henna from Marrakesh. I had already accomplished all three of my missions when the murder took place. It was a few days before the holy month of Ramadan. End of the day. The muezzin would call the fourth prayer at any moment. Doubtlessly afraid himself, he forgot to do it.

I knew the murderer. He had shoved me on his infernal run. A large, fairly strong man who wore a three-day-old beard. His clothes were dirty, stained with different colors of paint. His face, fairly handsome (a traditional beauty, like all of that which exists in Fes), inspired confidence despite all the anger that filled him. This was not the face of a murderer, it was more that of a pleasure-seeker, a man who smoked kif and who never fought.

All I knew of the victim was his voice, the last words before his death, before the final voyage: "Help... help... he's going to..." The voice that knows, that sees death racing toward it to suspend its breath and silence it forever.

The murderer had ripped the man's stomach open, intestines were spilling out from the side and were scattered on the ground. Blood spilled out too, hot and very red: the image was precise, clean, just a few words had brought it to life in my mind, in my head which did not know what to do with it. An obsessive image.

A knife in the stomach, is that all it takes to kill, to make someone die? I had trouble believing it. But all the voices around me were categorical: he really had died, by a single blow. An economical, very quick death.

And the murderer, the painter, where was he? He had disappeared. Fled? Already captured by the police? I asked a man selling slippers. He answered quickly, thrilled to inform me: "The secret police have arrested him." Since I said nothing, he added: "I thought there was no secret police in Morocco anymore. But this murder proved me wrong. They couldn't stop him from killing, but they captured him right away. Right now, he should already be at the police station at Bab Ftouh. On the other hand, the body is still there... Have you seen all the flies that have suddenly appeared? They love cold flesh... And of course, the ambulance won't be here for an hour... Nothing has changed in this dump, that's for certain." He'd given me more information than I expected. I thought I knew everything then. Before leaving, an essential question popped into my mind and I asked him "Why did he kill him? You must know..." He paused a moment before answering me, very disappointed, very sad to have no answer: "I'm very sorry, but I don't know. Only God must know! And the police, eventually..."

As I had no morbid curiosity, I avoided looking at the body bathing in its own blood. I was much more concerned with the fate of the painter. I had seen him, he didn't have the face of a murderer. I felt no pity for him but rather tenderness. I was intimately convinced that he had been pushed to act in that extreme manner. I wanted to know more about him. To see him again. Defend him. I was on his side, despite myself.

He had disappeared. He too was gone for good. He would not be hung, the death penalty doesn't exist in Morocco. As I left the city with my French friends, I thought about his fate, his future life in prison. Of that other life that would soon begin for him. He would not be executed—I repeated those happy words to myself. I was relieved, but I didn't know exactly by what or how.

"He will be alive. I will return to Fes."

Leaving the Fes medina when you don't know it well is a real nightmare. We asked the Fassis to guide us. They did it willingly. And each time we found ourselves at an impasse again. We were lost too. Again, we asked people for the path out of the labyrinth. In vain. It took us over an hour to find ourselves at the city gates, an hour of turning around, walking like the blind. An hour to finally be able to breathe deeply and say: "We're saved! We're not crazy!"

The painter stayed with me as we drifted. His story spread quickly throughout the city. The image of the knife stuck in the victim's belly came up most often in conversations and each time it evoked horror. People said "The painter from Derb Chrabliya stabbed his colleague. His intestines spilled out of his stomach." These two sentences repeated themselves, with variation of course, from shop to shop, from one passerby to the next, and from neighbor to neighbor. And the closer we got to the medina's exit, the clearer the story became. This is how I came to know that the painter had stabbed his colleague over five dirhams, which the latter had been demanding for two days. The painter, who was fairly poor, begged him to wait for the end of the week. The colleague didn't want to hear any of it and continued to demand the five dirhams all day long. After a time, it came to blows. Infuriated, beside himself, the painter took a large knife that he always kept in his took box just in case, and brandished it to frighten his colleague. The latter, provocative, changed his tune. "Kill me! Go ahead, kill me! I'm not scared of you. Kill me if you really are a man. Go ahead, kill me with your big knife. I'm not scared..." The painter took him at his word and took off behind him through the streets of the medina. It was at that moment that I met him.

22.

A Night with Amr

I don't know Amr. I've never met him. Until three days ago, I didn't even know he existed. All it took was my friend Alain showing me a photo of him and he suddenly entered my life, gently, like a sea breeze blowing in over Rabat and Salé on a July evening.

All week I've been burning. Rushes of heat, which tortured me in Morocco and which I shared with my mother, M'Barka, have returned to my body. Once more I am filled, day and night, with anxiety. Fear. Isolation. Money troubles. The pains of the heart. And love, which I seek and which hurts me each time. I know it all too well: love is difficult, so difficult, but I pursue it, desire it. I may be a masochist.

When Amr arrived in my life, my Parisian lover was on the war path, attacking me, my way of living and seeing the world, my sensitivity and my antiquated beliefs. He placed logic before all else, constantly critiquing, commenting on everything and letting nothing pass unnoticed. I felt as though I had been robbed of my self, of everything Moroccan, Arab. I felt disturbed, jostled, assaulted. I couldn't understand anything anymore, doubted more than necessary, thought myself weak, inferior to the whole world. Luckily Amr, through this black and white photo, was with me. In the middle of the night, after a heated phone call with my lover during which we each hurt each other (I couldn't take having everything about me analyzed, labeled, so I attacked, I told him everything... the things I couldn't stand about him, my mental block, my shyness, my nonchalance, I verbalized the things that kept the relationship from working, my discomfort, my self-absorption, my sentimental fundamentalism), Amr called me. I picked up. I looked at him, took a close look.

In Morocco, Amr would be named Omar. I needed to Moroccanize him to better love him as an Egyptian. Amr is Egyptian. And so all I can do is love him. I've watched so many Egyptian movies and TV shows. Egypt occupies a vast space in the collective Arab imagination, deserts and mountains. In his photo, Amr appears as if in a movie, a movie that would be directed by Mohamed Khan or Yousry Nasrallah. He is looking through a window: he is looking at me. Short hair, like mine is right now. Huge eyes, softly deep and most likely black: a gaze filled with a touching, troubling sweetness and goodness. Something sad in his features, but also light; in him it is certainly an intelligent lightness: irresistible! I imagine how easy it must be to melt for him. He is handsome, handsome with a heat that is brilliant without dullness; handsome with sincerity, with the light of a starry night. One would be grateful to be with him, have him to oneself, even if for just a moment: beauty must always be joy, a source of joy. He gazes out the window wearing the faint trace of a little smile, the beginning of a smile that would certainly illuminate his face, relax his sensual lips, and hollow his cheeks out even more. Unlike many Egyptians, Amr is not fat. He is thin, thinness incarnate. A feminine thinness. He is elegant, meticulous, spends hours in front of the mirror dressing up, preparing himself, checking everything, putting on creams, gel, trying on different outfits indecisively. He intends to be the most handsome, the most charming, the one you love at first sight, who you want to get close to, the subject of each whim, the one you pamper. He deserves it. There is no question about it. He is aware of his power, his charisma, but he still doesn't abuse it. He gives, he gives of himself willfully without crossing certain lines. Something aristocratic.

Amr comes from a rich family in Cairo. They were not always kind to him. They would say wounding things to him, of the sort that hold you back from living, shouting them at him daily. They would scold Amr for being feminine, for not being the way they expected, for being different. They did not try to understand, they instantly condemned. They would insult him, humiliate him, poor Amr.

"Why are you like this?"

"Like this? Like what? I don't understand."

"You're not like other people."

"Yes, that's it. He's not like other people."

"Which other people?"

"You know, other boys... other men."

"But I'm not a man, at least not yet. I'm still a kid, I'm only fourteen."

"You'll need to change before it's too late. You can't keep acting like this."

"I don't understand. I don't understand at all. What do I need to change?"

"Don't speak like that. You sound like..."

"Who do I sound like?"

"You know."

"No, I don't. I don't know anything. Stop torturing me. Say what you have to say. Go ahead, out with it. How do I seem to you?"

"You know the way you speak, and your gestures, and your manners. Men, real men, don't act like that. They behave, they're manly…"

"But what do you mean when you say 'real men?' 'Real men' don't exist. That's all made up. They're made to believe that they're strong, they're told how to act, and they do it. They're there to perpetuate pointless rules and traditions. Men believe that they have the power. I don't want to be like them."

"So you'd rather act like a woman, is that it? The man's woman."

"Our mother spoiled you."

"It's none of your business. I am what I am. Go stick your nose in things that actually concern you."

"Of course we're sticking our nose in, you're putting our honor in danger, our reputation. You're going to change, whether you want to or not. We're the ones who decide."

Amr didn't change. He put up with the ridicule, the insults, the violence for two more years. He cried. He shouted. He argued with his whole family. They hit him. He protested: "Yes, I love men. I love them."

One day, he was gone. He left his family and their prejudices forever. He could no longer put up with their lack of respect for him. They constantly told him that he was sick. They disowned him, which was fine with him: he was finally entitled to peace.

He joined a group of boys like him. They understood each other, loved each other, helped each other out in life. There was Samir, Salim, Sobhi, Sarim, Tamer, and Essam. A gang who lived freely and refused to conform. Modern odalisques who spent most of their days lazing around like cats. Each of them had a man of a certain age, a man in his forties. They were kept boys and they didn't mind it one bit. "Why should we be bothered?" Amr would tell himself. "There's no reason to be. Money is just a means, and since there is so much of it, why should I tire myself out working like a slave, doing something that I don't like? Taking care of oneself is already a job, and it takes so much time. And then there's my man… The others can keep their opinions to themselves. The camel only watches his brother's hump, never his own."

Amr had decided to be happy, and at the same time, to make others happy, to take his time, to be lazy, to dream, to live the dream. He dreamt of becoming an actor.

In the middle of the night, he told me this secret. In exchange, I offered him mine: "Since I was a little boy, my life's dream has been to become a filmmaker. Life hasn't allowed me to make it come true. But I'm still working. It's my secret, don't tell anyone. One day, I will be a director and I will hire you as my lead actor. You will be my Mohsen Mohieddin. It's a secret, don't tell anyone… not even your man."

That night, I didn't succumb to sleep until dawn. The birds began to stir, preparing themselves for song. I fell asleep and Amr watched over me. He even took me on a tour of Cairo, to see its neighborhoods, Zamalek, Mounira, Dokki, Garden City, El-Helmiya, its saints, Sidna El-Hussein, Sayyida Zaynab, its bridges, and of course, its river: the Nile.

The next day, I awoke very late. I lounged about like a cat for a half hour. Amr, fresh and fragile, was still at his window, still wearing his lovely short-sleeved black shirt and his enigmatic half-smile.

23.

Oum Zahra Goes to the Movies

She's still alive, Oum Zahra.

She lives next door to us, in the neighborhood of l'Océan. Her home grows darker and darker. Everything she owns is in the bedroom: an old armoire where she hides her "treasures," a little color TV set, and photos hanging on the wall, the great majority of them in black and white. That's all she has, all she has left.

She spends her days alone with her cat, to whom she has given a peculiar name: Michmiche.

When she was young she worked for Christians. She often tells us that she had been very happy with them. They respected her, paid her well, and even sometimes brought her on vacations to Marrakesh. They taught her dignity, the meanings of freedom and independence. They didn't have children: they dedicated themselves to each other and truly loved each other. Oum Zahra regarded them fondly, and speaks of them with the same fondness, in her voice and her gaze.

She never wanted to marry, even when her Christians went back to France. "Why should I?" she would sometimes ask, "To be owned by a man who believes he's god on earth? To be his maid and prostitute, slave to a jailer who shuts me away in the darkness and feels that he has been vested with a divine mission: to protect values and traditions?" No no, she never desired that prison, that sacro-sanct institution. She would leave that to other women who accepted it with resignation.

She always welcomed men into her bed. They gave themselves to her willingly, they never stayed very long, they loved themselves in her and they left, happy, light, oblivious to the realities of the world for a few hours. She said "my men." They answered "dear Mistress." She said "when and where." They answered "whenever you wish, wherever you wish."

But now these men don't come to her anymore, they have forgotten her, they are dead or married with witches for wives. Has the Time of Love passed? Will it never return? Not so sure. She's probably over seventy. But last year she went out with a boy who was only thirty years old. People thought she was his mother, or even his grandmother. It scandalized the neighborhood. Let others say what they would, she did what she wanted, she followed her heart and her truth. The boy seemed to truly love her. Surely, he did love her. But now, he doesn't even come around anymore. Oum Zahra doesn't cry over him. She has replaced him with the soldiers from the military barracks, to whom she rents out rooms in her house. These military men are handsome. Sometimes they don't even pay rent, she doesn't bear a grudge, she keeps them close to her. "They have nowhere to go. They keep me company. I see them, I hear them and I feel them living beside me. And for that, I am grate-ful to them. They warm my house and that, that is priceless."

The Christians taught her to drink and to smoke, which she continues to do. She smokes a lot, only black tobacco, only a cheap brand, Casa Sport. But the kind she likes best is Troupe, a brand distributed only in military barracks. Every Saturday night she needs her liter of red wine. Sometimes I am the one who buys it for her. She says to me "My little Aziz, I won't have a good rest again tonight. You know what I need. It's the only thing I have left. Can you go get it for me?" She drinks it all by herself, throughout the night, while smoking cigarettes and listening to music, old French songs, Damia, Edith Piaf, Maurice Chevalier, and others. The whole neighborhood knows about these parties in which her soldiers gladly participate; it doesn't shock anyone. Some think she's disgraceful, crazy, but when they run into her they can't help but treat her with kindness. Because of her age, I think: one must show respect for the elderly. All the ladies in the neighborhood adore her cat, Michmiche (he also drinks red wine). Oum Zahra says he doesn't piss just anywhere, he uses the toilet too, all by himself, like a grown up.

Today, she is getting sicker and sicker. She suffers from pneumonia, which has worsened over time because she doesn't want to stop smoking.

At night, she sits in front of the television for hours. She loves American movies and hates Egyptian shows, which she finds boring. Sometimes, she dresses up and goes to the Al-Hamra cinema. Over time, the theater's patrons, all of them men, have grown accustomed to Oum Zahra's appearances. They don't bother her. They offer her cigarettes and sometimes ask her for a light. She has her spot in the tenth row. She lifts her head toward the screen and even before the movie starts, she begins to cry silently, tears, uninterrupted tears. She only goes to the theater when they show war movies: it's her favorite genre. They remind her of the son she had so many years ago with an Englishman, her son who died in the war in Indochina. War movies allow her to watch him live again and then die, run and then fall, light up from within and then burn out, laugh and then suffer, and in the end go off forever... far away from her, alongside the Chinese in the sky.

24.

Angels' Terminal

Tangier has been a desert since summer ended. The rare tourists filter out, fleeing the city as though terrorized by the ghosts of its past. There are hardly any angels left in Tangier. They have left this once international city, chosen other itineraries, other trains, other boats. Sometimes one or two of them can be found in the Medina, around the Kasbah, in Marchan or on the beach near the train station and the port. Fallen angels in disguise, clinging to old memories for survival. Paul Bowles is dead. Mohammed Mrabet watches over his grave, which may someday be as legendary as that of Jean Genet in Larache: a Muslim grave! The streets fill up with dogs without masters and cats that will forever be free. Also with men with scars. Every night, they meet in darkened alleys to drink bottle after bottle of cheap wine. These meetings often end in brawls; they pull out knives, shatter bottles, and butcher each other. Saturday and Sunday they are back in the streets by late morning, offering a chilling spectacle to passersby: bruised cheeks, fresh, red scars that have not been disinfected. Theirs is a shattered beauty, the consequence of broken dreams.

Many of M'Hamed's friends are scarred. Not him. He likes them, some days he follows them, but not at night. M'Hamed stayed in school all the way up to the baccalaureate. He had no desire to go to university. "What was the point?" he asked himself. "You give away all your time and energy and in the end, you're just another unemployed graduate." He decided he would wander about in life, in the city and, of course, in the blue sea. He dreamed of many destinies, dreams that crossed the Mediterranean and took root on the other side. He knows that Morocco will not give him what he wants: he has no chance here. No rich family to help him: just a mother who cooks for him every day and doesn't ask too many questions about life's direction; and a father who is always somewhere else, in his grocery store where he sometimes spends the night. M'Hamed is a prisoner at liberty, that's how he's always described himself.

He's 25 years old. He knows he's nice to look at, pleasing, especially to foreigners. Women, men. At first, he only approached women, approached them as a conqueror, sure of his means, sure of his power to seduce European girls (most of them natural or bottle blondes). These girls were used to men who didn't want to act like men and so they hungered for machismo. Because he knew they liked it, M'Hamed acted manly in an exaggerated way: he'd puff out his chest, darken his gaze, and make his soft voice lower, grittier. He did quite well, especially in bed: they all said he made love like a beast. He gave himself to them fully, hoping his efforts would bear fruit. Instead, promises, always promises. And then, just as quickly, they forgot him. Some of them would send a postcard or two, but no more. Each time, he felt betrayed, robbed, dispossessed.

"Why are these blondes all the same? In my arms, it's romance, pink and blue, anything goes, even sex without a condom. As soon as they leave, I stop existing, they deny me, kill me. And yet they are happy to send their friends, their boyfriends and the boyfriends' girlfriends my way so I can guide them around Tangier, show them the secret spots. They all say: we don't want to be tourists, we want to get to know the people, get close to them, speak to them, touch them… And so I help them, after all I have the time, and the days are so long here… I give them what they desire, I try to be funny and serve them. At night, the girlfriends all want me in their beds. And there too I have to be on top of my game, stay hard, give it to them rough, act like an Arab man. They all like it. This is all I am to them: a cliché they are happy to know is alive and well and offered up so easily. Best of all, it asks for nothing in return. I've never dared ask for a single thing. I always think that they will understand. They know the situation in Morocco, the difficulties, the many obstacles… But instead they're always whining, complaining about how exhausting their jobs are, how they miss the sun. They remind me how lucky we are, we Moroccans, to be so lively, so respectful of tradition, so authentic, real and stress free, far from the modern world. I don't dare contradict them, ruin their vacations, open their eyes to the truth that is right there before them but that they refuse to see… I have no choice. I imagine what they say to each other as soon as they get back to Europe: 'Oh M'Hamed! He's so handsome and charming, so nice, so sweet, we really can count on him!' But I'm sick of it, sick of everything. Europeans, Tangier, this country that forces its youth to sell itself, to prostitute itself to survive. I'm sick of it… so sick…"

M'Hamed noticed the man right away. He was standing in front of the Petit Socco with two short brunettes. M'Hamed took an immediate interest in them. He walked closer to them. They were speaking French.

"Do you think this is the Grand Socco?" asked one of the brunettes.

"No," said the man. His voice was soft and slightly sad. "I don't think so. It must be up ahead, this way. What do you think, Isabelle?"

Isabelle didn't answer. So M'Hamed jumped in, looking only at the man: "You're right, the Grand Socco is that way. It's a five-minute walk." All three were speechless, surprised, suspicious, wondering who he was. M'Hamed, reassured that the man was exactly as he'd thought, continued: "You're in luck, today is the weekly souk. The alleys are filled with merchants from all over the Rif mountains, selling their goods. You should go. You won't regret it, they have everything, even kif." And he left them, sure that he would see them again. He knew exactly where and when. Tangier is so small.

In the middle of the afternoon, at the time when the faithful left the mosque after the Al-Asr prayer, M'Hamed showed up at the Haffa café. The horizon was clear. The sea as blue as ever. Off in the distance, America, the Masters of the world, the United States. And there, Europe, so clear, so close you could almost touch it… The café was half-full. People pining for Paul Bowles and his friends sipped their mint tea in silence. It wasn't very warm but the sun was out, clear and calming, sheltering. It was October, the month of the dead. M'Hamed glanced quickly around the café. He saw the three French people and walked toward them without hesitation. He had it all prepared in his head.

"So, did you find the Grand Socco? Did you like it?"

Isabelle the brunette answered immediately, enthusiastically:

"Oh, it was magnificent! The women from the Rif were so beautiful in their pretty clothes. You were right, it's enchanting. Thank you for the recommendation. Would you like to join us?"

Unsettled, M'Hamed didn't know how to respond. His plan was working too quickly. He hesitated. Isabelle took up the charge.

"We would so love to speak to a real Moroccan. My name is Isabelle. And you?"

"M'Hamed. I know, cliché for an Arab."

"I'm Sophie."

"And I'm René."

"Pleasure to meet you. Are you all French?"

"Yes," they said in unison.

"Is this your first time in Morocco?"

"Yes it is, well, at least for us girls. But this is René's third time."

"No no, it's just my second. The first time was twenty years ago. Twenty years already, wow!"

"And do you like it?"

"Yes, we love it." They answered, again in unison.

M'Hamed went on questioning them. For a long time. The questions came to him easily. He wasn't playacting too much. The three French people were delighted to answer, to give their impressions.

René continued to watch him from across the table, studying his face and body. René was very tall and very thin. His blue eyes fascinated M'Hamed, who wished his own were the same color—he'd even began seriously considering buying blue contact lenses to look a bit European. René's insistent gaze reassured him. He started to feel happy, even to forget his plan. He had, of course, already slept with men, always Europeans. This didn't bother him. For René, who was falling deeper and deeper under his spell, he put all of his beauty on display. He lit up, strutting like a peacock. René was smitten, he nearly trembled with desire for the man from Tangier.

M'Hamed was beside himself with joy. He felt his dream could rise again.

Naturally, the three French people asked M'Hamed to have dinner with them the next day and he accepted their invitation. René was the happiest of all. The two girls understood the situation and had decided to help. And they liked M'Hamed too.

M'Hamed brought them to a popular restaurant in the heart of the Medina. They had broad bean soup with cumin and olive oil for an appetizer, fried fish and vegetables for the main course, and seasonal fruits and mint tea to finish it all off. It was all fairly cheap and they were surrounded by Moroccans. No tourists, aside from the three French people. M'Hamed introduced them to the cook and servers, all of whom he knew well. Then, after dinner, an obligatory stroll. It was nice out. M'Hamed suggested they walk down to the port, which they still had not seen. Then he brought them back to their hotel, The Rembrandt, Avenue Victor Hugo. The girls, who were very tired, went up to their rooms right away. M'Hamed and René decided to have one last drink in a café not far from the hotel—it was only eleven p.m.

"This is very nice, sharing this drink with you. Nobody goes to bed early in Tangier."

"I don't either. And what do you do, in this case, when you can't sleep?"

"I dream."

"Is that all?"

"That's a lot."

"True."

"The only way I can go on living, surviving, is by dreaming."

"What do you dream about?"

"The future, of course. A better future."

As they chatted, they slowly sipped their mint tea.

"I can't get enough of this stuff."

"We drink it all day long and, luckily, nobody complains."

"Do you live far from here?"

"Not really. A fifteen-minute walk."

"Alone?"

"No, I live with my parents. I'm an only child. My bedroom is on the second floor and they sleep on the first. I can bring friends over if I want. That's not a problem. I'm free. Do you want to come with me?"

René pretended to hesitate but eventually agreed. They left the bustling café immediately.

After a half-hour of walking, they still had not reached M'Hamed's house.

"Is it far?"

"No, not far at all. Just ten more minutes. You'll see."

René was not reassured.

"If it's still far, we can come back another day. I'm in Tangier until early next week."

"I swear, we're almost there. Do you see the house over there with the red shutters? That's mine."

M'Hamed's house was in a poor neighborhood on the outskirts of Tangier. All the houses there were still under construction. The streets were calm and dark, there were no streetlights. Danger could be lurking all around.

M'Hamed's parents were sleeping. He and René went right up to the second floor and entered the Tangerian's bedroom. It was barely furnished but clean: a small bed, two chairs, a yellow rug on the ground, with a little armoire and photos of Isabelle Adjani (his favorite actress) stuck to the walls. René immediately noticed a scent that filled the room. At first he couldn't tell where it came from, but then he realized that it was the scent of M'Hamed's body. His fears melted away. And he imagined embracing him, kissing him, M'Hamed's skin and the taste of him, that mouth, he wanted to press his own against it. He moved closer to him and put his right hand on M'Hamed's left cheek to caress it.

"What's Europe like?"

"Europe?!?"

"Yes, Europe. Paris, Madrid, London. It's different. It's better than this place, isn't it?"

"Better? I'm not sure. But yes, it's very different."

"Why do you come here? Why do you visit Morocco? What does it do for you?"

"I'm not sure how to answer. We come here for the sun, of course... to see the landscape, the monuments... the crafts... the handsome, charming people... like you."

"Is that all!"

"Morocco is a beautiful country. That's why we come here from so far away."

"Beautiful? Maybe to you, but it's not beautiful to us."

"You don't think your country is beautiful?"

"No."

"You don't like anything here?"

"No. I have nothing here—no luck, no future. It's a place where only the rich can live. For me, for the rest of us, every day is a battle and we never win. And we never will. So why should Morocco be beautiful? I don't see anything here for us. It's all for you, the tourists, the rich. Young people like me only have one thing on our minds: how do we get the fuck out? How do we escape and make money like you, like the rest, people with satellite dishes and private beaches in Tétouan? People here kill themselves every day by hiding in refrigerator trucks or taking off in makeshift boats under the cover of night. Everyday a dozen, if not a hundred of them die drowned, refrigerated, asphyxiated... It's all we talk about in Tangier. I don't have the courage to do what they do. I'm weak, and I will grow even weaker if I stay here. I'll go crazy, end up homeless, and nobody will wonder what happened to me. I will be just one more shadow. So I have to go away, far away… People will only pay attention to me in this dump once I'm rich, with lots of money in my pockets and in the bank like a drug lord. I have to go to Europe—to Spain, Germany, Italy—it doesn't matter where. Once I get there, I'll do what I can, I have friends all over these countries. I have to… And for that, I need your help. You have to help me. You're the only one who can help me. You see, I'm nice, poor, I don't harm anyone… Do you hear me? You're the only one who can bring me. You have to… It's the only gift you can give me for what I just gave you… my body… Do you understand?"

René wondered just where he'd ended up, he felt the fear surge up in him again. M'Hamed's eyes grew redder and redder as he spoke. He was serious. At the same time, he seemed out of it, menacing, prone to of all kinds of craziness.

"I'm talking to you. Do you hear me?"

"Yes, I hear you. What can I do for you?"

"What can you do for me? So many things. You're rich. France is rich. You can buy me if you want. I'll be your slave. I just want to go there, get rich, and come back here. It's not too much to ask. You'll tell them at customs 'this boy is my adopted son.' You can send me an invitation, a housing certificate… No, that won't work, the consulate won't give me a visa with that. Figure it out… All I know, all I want is to go to Europe, and you're the one who can make that happen. Here, I'm scum. My fate is in your hands. Do with me what you want. I'm yours and I want to go."

M'Hamed was crying, shouting. All his fears, all his demons continued to attack him. He was transfigured by despair. René remained paralyzed, unable to react, to say a single word, to sympathize. He dared not even move. They were two people in the night, each wrapped up in his solitude and selfishness.

Suddenly, a woman's voice:

"M'Hamed… M'Hamed… Is that you crying?"

"No, mom, it's the TV."

"Go to sleep son. It's late, go to sleep. May God open doors in front of you."

"Ok, mom. Good night."

"Good night, son. Did you drink water?"

"Yes, I even have a bottle from Sidi Ali in here."

Touched by the mother's words, René took M'Hamed into his arms at last, brought him to bed, and joined him.

The rooster crowed. The muezzin, with a smooth, sensual, eternal voice, announced the first prayer of the day. But the sun had not yet risen over Tangier.

25

First Return

Paris was beginning to empty out. As usual, the Parisians had been in a rush to leave for their vacations (in search of seaside sunshine) since early July. Even Barbès had nearly been deserted by its Arabs and Africans. My internship at a weekly magazine would begin in fifteen days. Returning to Morocco, or even thinking about such a trip, was not an option (especially not in the summer).

Leave Paris?

The city had completely engulfed me. I could no longer imagine myself outside of it. My new life was built in Paris, for better or for worse, depending on the day and the season. But in these second two weeks of July, it was mostly worse: I was overcome by an intense feeling of solitude, of abandonment. On a morning that seemed just like all the rest, I was hit by this frightful fact: I wasn't really important for anyone. I was completely alone in this city. Freedom didn't mean anything anymore, it suddenly lost all flavor. Left to my own devices, there was no accounting for what I might do. Paris is a dangerous city for solitary souls. Instead of supporting them, it pushes them deeper before letting go of them completely.

The weather was so lovely and I didn't have much money. Like many Parisians, I was getting by. Each day had its anxieties, questions that often had no answers: how would I make it, how would I even live? Sunshine wasn't pleasant in Paris. I would have preferred for it to be extremely overcast, for the sky to reflect my mental state, filled with clouds, grey, rainy. What I desperately needed was the lid that Paul Verlaine talks about in one of his poems. But the weather was beautiful and that was unbearable. Unlivable. I had to find protection from the sun, which mocked me all day long. In my little studio, I closed the blinds at midday. I needed darkness to return me to myself momentarily and bring me brief moments of calm. Intimacy needs darkness; it can't live in broad daylight. Sometimes I would go to the movies at night, but there was nothing interesting to see, only B movies, Z movies, trash... Even the movies couldn't help me: how far away the fall was! The Moroccan family from Agadir that lived across the hall from me wasn't even there. Lusty Arnaud was gone too. Love had only complicated my life, I didn't want it any more. I have always been able to spend long stretches of time without sex.

I was living through one of the nightmares of the capital. This frightening experience is an essential phase when you move to Paris, the big city. People had told me, I had been warned, but that didn't ease my pain. I had to confront the chasm on my own, pull myself out of it. Where would I go?

One answer came to my mind, insistently: Morocco! Escape to Morocco! Recover in Morocco?

With naturally little deliberation, I decided to follow this intuition, this unexpected plan, and give in to the pull that I'd forbid myself from acknowledging from the very beginning. Go back to Morocco after two years of absence? Return even though I still hadn't achieved anything? I still had nothing to show for it, not for my family or myself. Should I see Morocco again, my Morocco?

Once again, I felt fear in my intestines. To convince myself that it was the right solution, I told myself over and over that my mother, my M'Barka would protect me. I would answer Morocco's call.

Because I couldn't afford it, I wouldn't go by plane. The only thing left was the bus. There are many companies that run trips of this kind in Paris, but during that season, and especially on July 15, seats were pretty sparse. And yet I managed to find one with the company Ouazzani Euro-Maghreb. One seat: Paris to Rabat. No return.

The bus was filled with passengers when I got on. All Moroccans! It was just us. Before the bus even left Paris, we were already in Morocco. The atmosphere was Moroccan, working class. I had never met any of these people in Paris. I had no idea where they'd been hiding, what they were doing in France. It was as though they were still in Morocco: nothing had changed in them. They spoke loudly. They were excited. Celebrations awaited them in their villages, engagements, weddings, circumcisions, so many chances to shine, to be admired. To prepare themselves, they sang. They practiced so that once they arrived it would sound better. Nearly all of them knew each other very well: that's the impression I got looking at them. I could see that they were happy, they looked happy. Their returns would be triumphant, they had no choice. They knew how they would have to act in Morocco, showing off, putting their success on display. Instead of being overwhelmed by this fraud, this travesty, they had decided to laugh, to play the game. The ritual "summer return of our emigrants" was familiar to them: no surprises on the horizon.

The woman who sat beside me had only two topics of discussion, her piety (her "return to God, to the straight path, to the light") and her son who was studying at the elite engineering school in Paris. She was proud of him, sure that he would have a bright future ("Not in Morocco, of course!"). She was "secure" in her relationship with God ("I'm a good Muslim"). She knew that her place in heaven was assured. Luckily, she never asked what I did in life. Instead, she asked me the inevitable question: "You pray, right, five times a day?"

Behind us sat a mother and her daughter. Throughout the ride, they used this rare occasion of being seated side by side, glued to each other for many hours, to air their dirty laundry. It was all there. The injustice of a mother who had only ever loved her boys. The frivolity of a daughter who was no longer a virgin, who wore skimpy, indecent clothing, which the mother forbade her from wearing in Morocco ("I don't want a scandal!"). The academic failure of one of the sons, whom the mother had decided she would leave in Morocco this time ("That way, he'll see just how spoiled he is in France."). Of course the daughter did not agree: the way she saw it, leaving her brother in a country he didn't really know would be a crime, another injustice... These poor ladies didn't agree on anything. After only two hours on the road, the whole bus knew their life story down to the smallest detail. They didn't talk, they shouted.

The trip took two days and one night. The arrival in Tangier was memorable. When we passed through customs, the officers let us through without searching our luggage. Some of the women, happy, visibly relieved, let out a series of blaring youyous and sang joyously and intensely to the king: "Long live Mohammed VI! Long live our king! Long live our young king!" I had nearly forgotten, an important change had taken place in Morocco while I was away.

It was night. I could barely make out Tangier, a city that rises into the sky, still as proud as ever, still as beautiful amid all the stars.

The bus got back on the road to Rabat. Morocco was plunged into darkness, it slept. I didn't get to Salé until around two in the morning. My neighborhood, Hay Salam, was deserted. Only the cats were awake, watching over the night. My mother was at her window: she was waiting for me as she looked up at the sky. She shouted in the middle of the night "Abdellah! My son, is it really you?" I answered, "Yes, mother, it's me... it's me... like before."

Like before, she threw the key down to me. I opened the door and ran up the stairs to the second floor of our home.

To see my mother again.

I placed my head against her chest and cried a little as I kissed it. She prayed like before and took my hand to lead me to my old bedroom. "Since you left, this has become mine. Now, it is yours again."

My mother. She had become a bit smaller, a bit older, but she didn't have any wrinkles. The tattoos between her eyebrows and in the middle of her chin were still as blue as ever. Her eyes seemed a bit tired. Her knees still hurt. She walked heavily, almost shaking the floor, as she always had. Her wardrobe was still mostly filled with long, brightly colored shirts and the scarves that were constantly tied around her head.

Physically, little had changed about her. M'Barka overflowed with love for me and I accepted all of it, every last bit. But I had almost nothing to give her in return. I had brought a few little "Parisian" gifts with me (which I'd bought from the Tati at Barbès). They were so little that I was ashamed of them.

Of course, she had prepared a tagine for me (chicken with raisins). Of course, she had organized everything in the house for my arrival. And of course, she never stopped talking, giving me news about everyone. My older brother and his two wives, my little

(129)

brother and his wife whom nothing could please and who wanted to rule in my mother's place, my sisters, their husbands, their children, the neighbors, their children who had all, also, left the country... She went through the whole neighborhood, she had a thousand things to tell me, to transmit to me, to discuss. I ate and I listened, delighted and sad at the same time. The world had changed for my family, my neighborhood, solitude now seemed to be the fate of many people. Every man for himself, the government didn't do anything for the people... My mother had known this for a long time. This is perhaps why she had finally let me leave.

I left. Two years later, I still hadn't achieved anything. No steady job.

"What have you done these two years in France?"

I couldn't find the words to answer her, or to lie.

"Did you work?"

I finally said, "Yes, I worked. Just to get by, to be able to pay rent, to get around, to eat. I'm not rich... Not yet!"

She understood. She changed the subject. "And how have you been dealing with the cold? Cold is the source of all ills..."

I still hadn't gotten used to the European cold, but I didn't tell her that. "I wear long underwear and a heavy coat when I go out. Otherwise, the apartments are heated with gas or electricity... luckily..."

"And who cooks for you?"

"I do. I remember your movements in the kitchen. I do as you do, I make your food."

"Even couscous?"

"Yes, even couscous!"

"And laundry? How do you wash it?"

"There are machines for that. It's very easy. Practical."

"Good, good. I see that you are very organized. That reassures me a little… And women, have you followed my advice and avoided them?"

"Always, mother. Always."

"And your passport? Where is it?"

"It's in my bag."

"Are you crazy? You can't leave such an important document in your bag. Someone could steal it. Is your French residence permit inside?"

"Yes."

"Give it to me. I will give it back to you when you are ready to go…"

"What if the police stop me?"

"I'll take care of everything. Tomorrow, I will photocopy the first three pages. You'll take it with you every time you leave. You can't have your passport stolen. I hope that you are taking good care of your diplomas in France. Where exactly do you keep them?"

"In my little library, between the books."

"Is it safe there? Are there thieves in France?"

The night was nearly over. We were still talking. Especially her, inexhaustible. She wanted to know everything, down to the slightest detail. I answered almost all of her questions and then abandoned myself to sleep, happy, relaxed and tired at the same time, confident and anxious about what would come next, the next day.

Day after day, I noticed just how much the neighborhood had changed. Poverty had pushed all the young people to flee, and the those who didn't would do whatever they could to survive. Each of the neighbors had rented out part of their house. Other people had invaded Hay Salam, I didn't recognize everyone in the street. My playmates in forbidden childhood games had also left. The little grocery stores and vegetable stands had doubled, along with mint sellers. Only the fishmonger had no competition yet. For the rest, it was each man for himself. Anything was acceptable to fend off complete poverty, to put food on the table at least twice a day. Some girls, those who weren't yet married to an unemployed man, an ex-con, or a failure, became prostitutes in Rabat. Luxury vehicles would come pick them up in Hay Salam, they were very successful. Nobody around them could find fault with it, they let them do it, they provided for their entire families now. They had become men in place of the men. On Thursday, the eve of the holy day, they would come to the hamam to purify themselves like everyone else. There too, the multiplication principle had a strong effect. When I left, there had only been two hamams, now there were four. In Hay Salam, one certainly had options when it came to bathing.

After the endless greetings, the people I recognized and said hello to would all say sarcastically: "How wonderful, you haven't changed!" By that sentence, they meant: "Where is the car, the BMW? Where are your expensive, designer clothes? Your gold watch?" I really hadn't changed, because I hadn't gotten rich. Consequently, I no longer had a place with them. Henceforth I could only be rich, nothing else. I could get rich or not return.

I decided I would rather flee again.

First to the beautiful Kasbah of the Udayas, which overlooks Rabat and proudly gazes down at Salé, at the mouth of the Bou Regreg River, facing the constantly raging ocean.

Then to Marrakech, where the earth is red, to visit in one day each of the seven magical saints: Sidi Abdul-Aziz, Sidi Belabass, Moulay Abdelfid... Baraka, always the baraka.

And finally to Europe. Return to Paris, this time by train.

Before she said goodbye to me, my mother, who preferred not to accompany me to the train station, suddenly took off the sirwal pants she was wearing and gave them to me as a gift.

"Never wash them. From time to time, put them on for an hour or two, they will protect you… from evil."

As usual, one last word of advice, "And above all, stay away from women, they are the source of all misery! Look at what happened to your brothers because of them."

I let her speak, reassure herself about my life far away from her, with the Christians.

26.

Turning Thirty

I'm afraid.

    I'm not afraid.

    I'm strong, very strong, indestructible.

    As a child, adolescent, I was sick. Sick but alive.

    Today, in Paris, I'm alive but sick.

    I feel weak. I'm no longer able to sleep at night, so I think about Isabelle Adjani, about her singing voice. I'm ashamed, having spent years in France, seven years already, that Adjani's voice has replaced my mother's in my head. No, no, it's not that I've forgotten her, my mother, no, it's simply that everything in me comes from her, everything that I am is marked by her, her indelible imprint. I suffocate.

    I am my mother with the voice of Isabelle Adjani murmuring, humming a song. "Pull marine."

I died. Three times.

    The first time.

    In the middle of a summer afternoon, in Salé, in my neighborhood, Hay Salam, the angel of death took my soul, but only for a few seconds. I saw myself from above, a sleeping body, peaceful and blue. Did he have pity on me, this terrible white angel? Did God make a mistake? They ended up giving back my anxious soul at the end of those few seconds during which they discussed my fate in front of me, my days and years yet to come, my fate despite myself. And they departed for other destinations. I opened my eyes. Everyone at home was taking a nap, except my father. He was in my mother's place, at my bedside. He had understood, seen what had happened. He gave me his hand, I took it, I got up, and we went out into the streets, barefoot, to lovingly reacquaint ourselves with life and light again.

The second time.

I was playing alone at a dead-end of Block 15. On the cusp of adolescence and already abandoned by my childhood friends. Not knowing any better, I touched a high-voltage electric pole. Electrocution. I lost consciousness. It was instant blackness, beyond myself, without memory. For how long? I don't know. When I came to, I saw that the entire neighborhood (dozens and dozens of people, a crowd) was in our house. Crying for me. Even screaming for me. It was unfair, departing at such a young age. I got up suddenly. A man said, "Quickly, quickly, wash his feet, hands, and face with hot water … quickly, quickly … but not with cold water, mind you!" An ambulance arrived a bit later. The crowd of neighbors carried me carefully, slowly. They took me to Avicenna Hospital in Rabat. I was proud that I was going to be cared for in the most important hospital in Morocco. I was happy, for once people were truly going to believe me, take my strange body and its maladies seriously. My heart and its beating greatly intrigued the doctor, a white-skinned man, a Fassi. He took an x-ray, put his hand on my chest, on my heart, for a long, long time, he saw something that was happening in me that I had never had access to, he understood my body differently than I did, which intrigued me. He caressed my cheek. Played with my hair. And, before leaving, he leaned toward me and murmured a secret in my ear. He said, "Between the two of us … you have a strong heart, a heart for life…You will live a long time, my son! Get up!" He saved me, and I still remember his name quite well: Doctor Salah El-Hachimi.

The third time.

To get away from Hamidou, with whom I was in love although he didn't know it, I went to risk my life on the other side of the sea wall of Rabat's beach, toward the wild, pitiless waves. I stepped on a large, slippery rock. An enormous wave immediately plucked me with sweetness and violence to transport me to another world in its company. I didn't close my eyes, I was conscious, and in this movement toward the depths of the ocean and of death, I understood, I saw.

… Hamidou wasn't worth the effort, this sacrifice, it wasn't worth going to the trouble of changing his opinion about me. He didn't see me. I didn't exist for him. He had told me a few minutes beforehand: "You have normal skin, it's missing something … how strange!" Hamidou didn't love my skin. He didn't love me. I didn't believe in loving myself. Love, I read somewhere, is often criminal… I was still with and inside the wave. Just before it smashed onto the rocks, I don't know by what miracle, I grabbed something—a branch, I think. I grabbed it, held on, and waited for it to pass, to subside. Then I got out of the water. I was on the sea wall, walking. It was the month of August. The souk was on the beach. And there I was all bloodied, wounded in the chest, the arms, the knees, the nose. Blood red. People stopped to look at me. I wasn't afraid, didn't think I looked ridiculous, I wanted Hamidou to see me that way, for him to panic, to take pity on me, to regret his indifference toward me, to cry, to beg for forgiveness for the wrong he had committed against me, to be touched, to love me, finally…

And at that instant, instead of seeking revenge, I would have said to him: "Goodbye ... farewell ... I finally belong to myself, remain with myself ... I'm alive despite you, without you, far from you..."

Two years ago, in Paris, Tristan came into my life. Today he's almost six years old. A little man. The little prince. I pick him up outside his school four days a week. I take him back to the large house, as he calls it, a huge apartment next to the Blanche subway station. I play with him. I make him do his homework. I give him his bath: he is completely naked before me, unself-consciously nude. Together we watch cartoons, *The Lion King*, *Finding Nemo*. Sometimes I tell him Moroccan stories, about my terrible young childhood, I teach him words in Arabic. We pretend to fight, sometimes for real. We cry, scream, mock each other, kindly, meanly. Each day he gets a little bigger, grows rapidly like a flower that one waters with care, with love. He grows before my astonished, wondering, happy gaze. Even when he annoys me, even when he acts like a little macho man, Tristan remains a little sun for me. The Parisian sun that will never burn my skin.

I repeat in my head what he'll say to his friends later, perhaps to his children: "When I was little, my babysitter was Moroccan, his name was Abdellah." Three hours a day, I play a small role in his life, in his future, and that makes me proud in spite of myself. I feel like I'm accomplishing a mission with him. I accompany him.

Tristan is not my son. Tristan is a little angel who sometimes cries like that, for no reason, he cries in my arms, I console him tenderly, but I never know about what. I'm envious of his innocence, his pure outlook on the world. He doesn't know. He still doesn't know. Ignorance is bliss!

There are some truths about me and about the world that I hope are never known. I reflect too much. I complicate everything, everything. I think, I think, a permanent bottleneck in my head. Ideas and images I don't know what to do with.

I'm so tired of myself, of being me in this hurried life. I look for something that will come, that is slow in coming. I should take a step, just one more, I should renew myself, find or summon the energy. I have plans: they tell me I always must have some in order to find a daily rhythm, a connection between the visible and the invisible.

The meaning of life, of my life, escapes me.

Others seem to be happy. Are they truly happy? What makes them happy? Why do they know where to go and I don't?

My name is Abdellah: the slave, the servant of God. I freed myself from Morocco's constraints (but really?). All that remains is to escape myself.

I looked for loneliness. I found it, and it's insufferable. I'm permanently myself, unable to forget who I am. My consciousness of my being has accrued over time. An anguished consciousness. I know what's happening inside myself, my beating heart, beating unevenly on occasion, my ears whistling, blood sometimes hot, sometimes cold, the air that produces a strange music while entering and leaving my nostrils, my cracking bones, my changing skin, the feuding ideas in my head, the jostling images in my eyes, and my sexuality that cries out its desire, yet I do not obey it.

The past few months, I've been haunted by the idea that I might go crazy someday. That seems easy to me today, to switch over to another mind-set and completely forget its other skin. I always loved the insane ones in Morocco. They seemed to be in harmony with the country. Are they still?

Death and madness possess me.

Last July, Dostoevsky and Genet became my favorite writers once again. They speak to me. We're afraid together. We go hand in hand toward life, tormented and sometimes miraculous, together, alone, each in his own terrible and delicious solitude. They can do nothing for me. I am possessed by them.

I must change my first name. Karim? Farid? Saïd? Habib? I am neither generous, unique, happy, nor loving. Wahid, then? Yes, definitely, at this moment I am Wahid, solitary and proud, susceptible and unhappy.

I'm headed toward something in Paris, that luminous and exceedingly quiet city. I walk toward my fate, and each day I have the impression that I'm not deciding anything. I'm not my own master. I took a step, coming to Europe, and I was swept up in the infernal movement of Western time. Everything passes quickly, all is quickly forgotten, everything is orderly, apparently clean, everything in its place. Everything is parceled out.

Today, I know, I pay the price.

It began with a slight despondency, nothing serious. I got over it, I had to get over it. Now it's started again, it's coming back but in another guise: crises of anguish, of panic. A red image, a taste in my mouth, a hemorrhage in my head. I anticipate falling. I see myself fall, a motionless body in the Parisian street that passersby pay no attention to. I wait and wait. But I don't fall. I'm still upright. I don't know where my strength resides in me, I don't know how to locate, guide, channel, define it.

The past few months, I'm no longer myself, I don't recognize myself. I look at my face in mirrors, I look at my feet, my hands, my nails, my hair, my skin, and each time I ask myself the same question: Whose are they?

In psychiatry, what has come over me, is happening to me, has an exact name: depersonalization.

Does becoming an adult mean being able to find the medical name for one's neuroses?

Tomorrow is my birthday. I'll be thirty years old. This I've decided: I'm going to enjoy looking at myself in the mirror, I'm going to masturbate deeply, aroused by my image. Thus will I be able to rediscover myself, perhaps, body and soul creating anew the sacred union of my being.

Tomorrow I'm going to be on another path, a way that leads to this other number: thirty-one.

I dream, I close my eyes for a few seconds, I close them violently, masochistically. I go blind. I open them, I'm elsewhere, myself in another age, older, in an indefinable time. This other world will certainly exist in my forties. I imagine it. Each day I create a long movie about it.

I've known this since my childhood. I'll be a forty-year-old man. Not sooner. Forty years in order to finally say, comforted, lighthearted, perhaps free: I am the man of my desires.

27.

The Wounded Man

We had broken our fast about two hours ago. It was getting dark.
Et Hay Salam was unusually calm. It was as if all the inhabitants of
this working-class neighborhood in Salé had suddenly moved to the
other side of the Bou Regreg River, not far from the beach in Rabat,
everybody who lives here, except for my family. The place was
deserted. It made you think that something extraordinary was about
to happen, something that would drastically change the entire
country, disrupt the land and the people still on it. A huge thunder-
storm that would bring hope, rain and a successful harvest. Or else
the Apocalypse: the end of the world, starting right now.

My mother, M'Barka, was sound asleep.

Ramadan was an exhausting month for her. Even though fasting
made her very tired, on a daily basis and all by herself, she had to prepare rounds of sweets, crêpes and, of course, *harira*, a soup she always
loved very tart with lots of tomatoes and lemon juice. In the past, my
sisters were happy to help her make every day of this holy month a
spiritual and gastronomic celebration, a never-ending ceremony.
Now the house was empty. Three floors with nobody living there.

Everyone had gone off somewhere, somewhere far away, some
other city, some other country, left for another world, to live there
among strangers, people I'd never know and never really accept.

The only ones left in the house were my mother, my younger brother, Mustapha, whom we almost never saw, and me. M'Barka was afraid to be alone now, quite often afraid, and time and again she'd repeat herself by telling me how solitude is a slow and dolorous poison.

That always made me sad, very sad. I never managed to completely share her suffering. On the other hand, I felt like crying every time I heard her talk like that. Every day, she would beg me not to tarry in the city once my classes ended at Rabat University, plead with me to come home early, before it got dark, beg me to catch the early bus and get home fast so the house seemed full again, so I could keep her company, help her get through her everyday tasks, cheer her up just by being there, put some life back in her, share a warm moment, make us feel like a family again before night fell.

At night, just when it came time for us to separate again, she'd never want me to retire to my bedroom. She'd want me to stay there beside her until she had fallen asleep. Sleep was death. And since my father's brutal disappearance one year ago, she suffered from bouts of fear and panic attacks. That's when she'd cling to me. She used to sleep in the living room, where the television was king. She didn't like that "apparatus," as she called it, but it wound up being the companion who got her through the day, this machine that emitted sounds, voices that somewhat reassured her, though not all the time.

Thanks to the price of satellite dishes coming down, we had just started to pick up the French channels, the ones that really interested me. When I could get it, I really liked watching Arte.

That channel made me think of myself as someone important: this intellectual and with-it student who was interested in things that people around him found boring or hard to understand. I was proud. I acted proud, like I was one of a kind.

That's the part I was playing that night, after I devoured a good amount of the delicious Ramadan food my mother made. I turned on the television. There was this movie on Arte.

I missed the beginning. Locked in the bathroom of some train station, Jean-Hugues Anglade was crying his eyes out. Obviously, he felt abandoned too. He was battling something as well, maybe solitude. I was instantly moved by him, by the actor and by the character he portrayed. Thanks to my knowledge of movies, it only took me about a minute to recognize that film, one I'd never seen before. It was *The Wounded Man* by Patrice Chéreau. A French film from 1984. A cult film. Something off-limits.

My mother was sound asleep. And right there on the screen, they were showing this movie that no one in Morocco could do anything about, whether that meant stopping it entirely or interrupting it to give a lesson in religious morality to this young hero who lived beyond the rules, wore his hair a little too long, and loved other men. This hero who was in love with one particular man.

I was faced with a dilemma. Faced with desire. Ready to watch that movie right to the end.

Watch it with my stomach knotted with fear. Constantly on the look out. My mother, asleep in back of me, could wake up at any moment and catch me in the act. Then she'd know my secret, my one big secret, know about my other life, the object of my desire. She'd make a big deal out of it. The whole thing would be a scandal. I'd be so ashamed, I wouldn't know what to do, what to say to her.

My stomach hurt. I ate too much when we broke our fast and couldn't digest it all. I was aroused by the level of desire that permeated the film, that had taken over Jean-Hugues Anglade and the other characters. It was the only thing they lived for, the only thing that kept them alive: sex, love and the danger that went with them. They'd feel attracted to someone, approach him, try to pick him up, flatter him to no end, pay for him, play with his head, rape him, toss him aside, kill him little by little. I was fascinated, hypnotized by what I was seeing. And I wanted to live like one of those characters, to be just like them. Outside the law. I wanted to love just like they did. Love another man. Just one. Alone. Illicitly. I wanted to touch myself. Stroke myself.

Lick myself. Bite myself. I wanted to go right up to the toughest one and give him everything I had.

My stomach was heaving. My sex was getting hard. And I didn't know what to do because I was still afraid in spite of the level of desire the television beamed right at me, this urge that overwhelmed me and soon drove me almost crazy.

Now my mother was snoring. Regular exhalations, loud snoring one minute, quiet snoring the next. But once or twice she stopped. I changed the channel immediately. I couldn't help taking this cessation as a sign that she was returning to consciousness, about to wake up and catch me watching this banned movie. Somewhat reassured after waiting an endless minute and turning towards her to make sure her eyes were completely shut and she was still miles away from me and all those images, I went back to watching *The Wounded Man* and his story. And suddenly my desire became uncontrollable and my fear came to the forefront.

Jean-Hugues Anglade was in love with this tall, handsome guy I seem to remember was dark.

A little like Gérard Depardieu in the early eighties. This virile, sensitive, hard-edged, merciless man.

A king. A dictator. A pimp.

Anglade fell for him the minute he saw him. And from that moment on, life revolved around this man who made him forget everybody else. No one else would ever matter as much as he did.

Almost from day one, he gave up everything, his former life, his family, just to chase after this guy. He'd turn up on the street, in train stations, in parking lots, trail after him, pursue him, clumsily try to seduce him, anything to have a minute of his time, a minute of his body. To have him love him. And it never happened. Anglade lived on passion alone. The kind of passion that could only be heartbreaking and tragic.

Patrice Chéreau's film, in the same tumultuous and brutal way it took hold of me that night and has remained forever in my mind, is extreme in the way it depicts the exacerbation of romantic feelings, extreme in the way it reveals how sex dominates the body. This film comes complete with slaps to the face, quarrels, pursuits, every kind of trafficking, tears, orgies, blood, sperm, down and dirty moments, obsessions and death. It shows the never-ending slide of a young man with blood on his hands, a man doomed from the start, toward this crime he commits for love.

I forgot his first name. He was the one I identified with. In love and frustrated, just like him. Ready to give up everything for some wild dream, some rock of a man, some emotion rarer than hen's teeth, some exceptional human being. And constantly afraid. Constantly in hopeless pursuit of the only person I desire. The man I love. The man the Americans call "The One." One man and one man only. Someone older than me so I could learn something from him, relive parts of the past with him, become this couple people wouldn't recognize. A spiritual leader, a master, a baker, a man of God who prays five times a day, an enlightened man, a parent, an uncle, a cousin…

The film played out in front of me, and lodged its force, its hopelessness and its religion in back of my eyes, in back of my mind. Without even knowing it, I had become a believer, someone prone to indulge in this lifestyle on a regular basis, someone adept at perceiving, at wandering about, at banging into bodies, at exploding with joy before I went crazy, even beyond crazy. What was forbidden stood right there in front of me, touching my scrawny and suddenly emboldened body. And what was forbidden stood right in back of me too.

I kept getting harder and harder, my heart even more confounded. My eyes were turning red. I was both happy and sad. Fired up and chilled to the bone, as if some gust of northern air, some blast from Tangier had passed over me. At one point, I wanted to wake my mother up and get her to look at these images, get her even more involved in this movie that moved and, for that matter, totally overwhelmed her well-mannered son. Wanted to move in towards her, snuggle up to her, find room on her lap, lift her hand to my stomach, feel her breath on my back, on my neck, recognize her smell in my nose and against my skin. Wanted to go back to where I began, the first door, the first opening that brought me into this world, that let me find life and light.

And there, back in the place where it all started, back at my original threshold, I'd hollow out a space, a depression and sit there crying while I watched this wounded man, this young man, this brother disoriented by love's searing intensity, sit there crying, crying over him and right along with him. Wanted to gently move my mouth across his eyes, slowly run my tongue across each one until I finally drank the slightly salty water that flowed from them and ran down his cheeks and across his skin.

I knew just what he was going through. I dreamed about it. Fantasized about it. I stopped thinking. Couldn't think anymore. My eyes hurt, my thighs hurt, my knees hurt, my sex hurt. I snapped out of it. The wounded man was still walking the Way of the Cross that all lovers walk. That's where this hero would fulfill his destiny, right here in front of us, here in this house that had no father, here in our almost empty living room, here in the privacy of our lives, so filled with silence and obscurity.

I used to think I was sophisticated, but, as I watched Patrice Chéreau's movie, I realized for the first time what an inexperienced movie fan I really was since I watched all movies the same way I always did. And by that I mean, the way I watched them back when my childhood years were ending and, still programmed by others, the religion of Indian films and Chinese Karate movies became part of my life forever. I started to rediscover myself. I guzzled images in dark and public theaters, sitting there with prostitutes and thugs. And those images delivered me from the shackles of my homeland, linked me to an art form that little by little gave me a reason to live, a way to see above and beyond things. I could leave the world, go beyond its gravity, see my own nakedness, then return to fight my battles.

I was in the heat of battle. In full revolt. Just days away from Ramadan's holiest night.

Suddenly my mother's music stopped. Not a sound came from her mouth, no wheezing, no humming, not a single breath. Was it Apnea? Was she dead, beyond all fear, no longer afraid, gone off to join my father? Was she awake now? Was she sitting there with me watching *The Wounded Man*? Would she figure out what these strange scenes meant, these pictures from another world, these images from hell? Was she suddenly going to jump up and start yelling at me, yelling in that voice she always used when things turned ugly, start pulling my hair, punishing me, pinching me, cursing me out? Would she try to castrate me right then and there?

With my heart in my throat, I turned to face her. Her eyes were open but she was staring at the ceiling. She was dreaming. She was still entangled in the sequence of images that sprang up in this dream that only she cultivated. Somewhat at ease, I changed the channel and asked her, in a quiet voice brimming with respect, if there was anything she needed. Her response was immediate, as if she had been preparing it for a long time, had fallen asleep thinking of it.

"I'd love a glass of water, honey!" I ran to the kitchen to get her one. She was very thirsty, had just returned from some long voyage. She wanted another one. "I will die, child, if I don't have have another one...Oh, my sweet son, may God..." She didn't have to ask me twice. I almost ran back to the kitchen, already happy that she would pray for me, remember me in prayers that were always the same, prayers that pictured heaven as someplace real and not some fictitious abode.

Her thirst quenched, M'Barka went back to her sleep, back to tending her dreams. But right before closing her eyes again, she gave me this blessing that absolutely bowled me over and still does: "My son, you need to watch, watch what you want on television...I will not get upset...Watch what you want..."

I turned the sound down and waited for my mother to start snoring again before I went back to watching *The Wounded Man*, finally catching up with the film's wounded hero. By now, he had completely run out of patience, was tired of love that cruised a one-way street, tired of humiliation, tired of aimless wandering and all that time, crazed with love, crazed. He was almost at the point where his path to crime would end, the moment, that single and final moment, when he'd have his way with the other man, finally possess the object of his desire.

Only death and that hit-man could give meaning, purpose and structure to this young man's tragic story, to his sublime love.

Naked, pressed against the man he loved, he was strangling him with his bare hands, snuffing him out while he made love to him. That's how he gave him everything he had: his body, his heart, his mind, his skin, his blood, his breath. He gave up his life by taking the life of the man who, right up to the end, refused to unite with him in that great religion of feelings and shared embraces.

It was tragic.

Love, like life, which at certain miraculous moments burns with light and intensity, is a tragedy. I knew that, knew it intuitively. I was twenty years old. *The Wounded Man* taught me that, taught it to me once and for all. I had been warned. The choice was mine. Would I give up? Never.

At the end of the movie, the credits flashed in front of my eyes. The name Hervé Guibert came up. He was the guy who wrote the script along with Patrice Chéreau. I had forgotten about him. This movie, this story, they were his too. Part of his life. The way he lived. A lifestyle I discovered and came to love when I read his books. He'd been dead for four or five years now.

Tears started running down my cheeks. Finally. But, why was I crying? Who was I crying over?

I didn't exactly know what to say, couldn't really answer my own question. Was it for Hervé Guibert, this man I knew inside and out after reading all of his books? Was it for the hero who in the course of that movie turned into a criminal, a brother, a friend, turned into me? Was it for my father who left too soon, who never got to see my life become a book, a story put into writing?

Was it for life itself, life, that when you come right down to it, is sad and terribly lonely despite what happiness Ramadan brings?

Even today, I still don't know. Even today, I still cry when I think of what actually happened back then, think about how the movie ended, think about Guibert, think about myself…and think about my mother who cried out in silence. And I cry for all of us.

The next day, I woke up very late. I only had one thing in mind. I was in a big rush to find my favorite cousin, Chouaïb, the cousin I was sort of in love with. I ran off to find him, seduce him, corrupt him. I hurried off to hang all over him, talk him into breaking the fast before sunset, breaking it by letting both of us talk about sex. Then we'd climb that hill in Bettana, his neighborhood, and from up there, right next to the old cemetery, we'd be able to see the opposite shore of the Bou Regreg River, see Rabat, the Hassan Tower, the Kasbah built by the Udayas, the public beach where poor people swam. Both of us would smoke a little hash. Then I'd put my head on this thighs. And in that state of silence and contemplation, I'd tell him all about the movie last night and gently, but directly, invite him to sin, to transgress.

To deliberately sin.

God would be watching us.

We'd do it anyway. Right through to the end. Right down to the sea. Right up into the sky.

Unlucky, one day I'd be unlucky in love, just like *The Wounded Man*. In the meantime, Chouaïb, this cousin with a moustache, this bad boy with a body big enough to wrap around mine, has a place in my heart and that's how I drag him off to the movies almost every day, then sit there under the bright lights, my eyes completely shut.

28.

The Chaouch[1]

My dear Adnane,

I am going to remember with you. Let's take off our shoes. Go out into the street. I'll take you by the hand. Restore the bond we once shared. Cross through death with you, this morning that is still night. The death of the father. My father. Mohamed. Do you remember this man, your grandfather? Can you tell me about him, whisper him in my ear? Tell me because I'm a bit lost these days: I've lost the image of this father, his presence, his trace. Give him back to me, this father who I knew without really under-standing him, without grasping him. Open up my memory, rummage through it, and find him for me. Where is he? Where is he sleeping now? What is left of him in my heart, my mind, my slightly blackened soul?

Adnane! Adnane, are you sleeping? Do you want to take a nap? No, please don't. Stay on this earth with me, under this exiting summer sun... Stay...

You are young. You have grown a lot, but you are still young. Still a child? How old are you now? Sixteen. Sixteen! A little man.

---

1. In North Africa, a name given to lower level public servants. From the Turkish word for "messenger" or "servant."

(151)

I see you. Amid all the words that are descending upon me, I see you. You approach life with the power of your youth, the remnants of your childhood. Do you still cry? Sometimes?

I envy you. I envy your eyes, which know still everything with freshness. I envy your skin, which is darker than mine. I envy your memory, there where I left it, as I've kept it. I want to find it again. Your memory. My memory. I'm asking you, begging you: plunge into me! Go to the bottom of my being and search for my father with me! Run, run! Swim, swim! Fly, fly! In the darkness of my heart, with your help, I want to see my father again. Confront him, gentle and violent. I want to see him like you, through you, close up, the way I never did.

I want to question him at last. Interrogate him. Reveal him. Read him.

Why did he leave us on that Friday in 1996? What was it about that spring Friday, the first day of spring, March 22?

Why did he leave us once and for all at the age of 66?

Dead. That's what they said, Adnane. That's what I saw. But I can't quite seem to believe it. My father, dead! Impossible.

I cling to this idea, to the impossibility of it, to my legitimate disbelief, my obstinate refusal. At this very moment, this morning that is still night, I am beside my father, my father's body. I lean toward him without daring to touch him and I speak to him. I murmur strange, nonsensical words in another language.

Adnane, you were barely five or six years old. You kept your distance that day, you remained in Agadir where your parents were living. We wanted to protect you. We didn't want to tell you or let you see anything. To keep from frightening you?

We were wrong, infinitely wrong.

Since that day, has anyone told you about your grandfather, about his history, his decline, his tenderness and his stifled anger?

Did your father, my brother Abdelkebir, tell you the story of our family name, Taïa, and the questions that surround it? Do you know about your grandfather's original tragedy? Do you have any sense of the utter humiliation he suffered his whole life, which kept him from picking himself up and which surely must have hastened his final departure?

No. Are you sure? No?

Then I will tell you. You need to know. Your father will get mad at me again and think that I've meddled in things that are none of my business… Don't worry about that… I know in my flesh, in my heart, that silence kills. Little by little. Through general indifference.

What happened to your grandfather… What carried and crushed him at the same time… Where do I begin?

He died before I could know him from within, before he could tell me with his own words what they did to him, what they took from him, what they imposed on him. I saw him weeping, pulling at his hair like a woman. But I never dared to ask him any questions. Approach him and listen to him, wait for his words, which were on their way. I never asked him anything… Nothing… This is the tragedy, Adnane. This is death. To live a whole lifetime at a person's side without speaking to him, without having the courage and the generosity to bare oneself before him. Why? Out of modesty? Out of respect? No, out of stupidity. Moroccans are masochists: to this day, they impose obsolete traditions on themselves that were invented by unknown people many centuries ago… Traditions that are said to represent the spirit of our country, the spirit of Moroccans, when they merely crush it, stamp on it day after day… Yes, my little Adnane, this masochism is what prevents us from existing, from communicating, from understanding, from opening our eyes. I don't want you to be a masochist. You are sixteen years old: all is not lost, you have time before you, to change, to get away, to see things differently, to critique the values that they have forcefully instilled in you.

Excuse me, Adnane, excuse me for speaking like this. Don't look at me like I've gone mad. Maybe you don't understand all that I am saying, the message I am trying to get across... I will try to be more straightforward. Direct. I'll return with you to your grandfather. My memory. My resentment. The end of the world. Friday, March 22, 1996.

I was at his side. I didn't cry. I spoke to him in fear and fervor. I wanted to resurrect him with my words. I was sure that his soul had not yet left the house. There still had to be a way to keep it there, to return it to my father's body. Coax it. Corrupt it. Like Faust, make a deal with the devil for it. So I spoke... I spoke quietly so that my mother and sisters who were crying in the other rooms would not come to disrupt my ceremony, my working miracle. I spoke, I spoke for an eternity.

I spoke. I said. I prayed. I loved. I gave. I read the Koran. The Hadiths, poems. I reinvented spirituality. I remembered the djinns, the saints: I invoked them all, each and every one of them. I played doctor. Nurse. Lover. Son. Little child. Baby.

I called out to God. I held out my hand. For a long time.

Nothing... Nothing came... We had been abandoned, my father and I. What could I do then? Continue to deny reality?

I violently shut my eyes. I tried to remember this father of mine in a happy moment. I searched. I searched like a madman lost in a labyrinth.

Day broke. The muezzin would recite the call to prayer five times. The world would learn the news. A father is no longer here with us. The chaouch of Hay Salam, which has always been our neighborhood, is dead. Mohamed Taïa. 66 years old. Only 66 years old?

No, no, I couldn't let that happen. I had to do something more. Shake myself up more. Demand the impossible. Whatever I did, I must not cry. A miracle. A miracle of strength. A miracle that came from another place, from the other world, one from the other religions. I was ready to do anything, even become an infidel, for my father. To abandon my convictions.

I opened my eyes. I leaned forward and, like a fireman, I performed mouth to mouth on him. Gave him my air. My exhalation. Gave him all that I am. Blood. Warmth. Fever. A breath. Life. God. His son.

I exhaled. I exhaled. I exhaled.

I tasted my father. For the first time.

I got up. I looked at him. A large, foreign body lying on a red rug. I saw him without knowing who he was, without recognizing him. He was mute. He was no longer breathing. His eyes were open: they were looking somewhere else. Where?

I stopped time. I stopped my heart.

I went crazy. I wanted to rip off my clothing. I did it. And, like my mother, I shouted. I screamed. I wept without tears.

I was not weeping for him.

I did it for me.

My father, Adnane, I killed him. I killed your grandfather.

From 1992 to 1996 he was ill. Gravely ill. His illness was contagious. The others said: we have to protect the children, by all means.

They separated us, took us away from him.

From 1992 to 1996, I didn't see my father.

When he was brought to the Océan hospital, the others said: Watch out! Nobody ever recovers from this illness. We still have to protect the children, still…

They protected us. They turned us into hardened criminals.

For the last two years of his life, he slept alone on the third floor of our house that was still under construction. There was only electricity in one room: the one where we'd tossed him. There was nothing in that room, nothing or nearly nothing. A yellow mat. A tiny bed. A small radio. A small television. Three books in Arabic. And the void all around.

This is where he lived out the last months of his life. Cold. Exile. Hell. Paradise?

I didn't say anything. I didn't do anything. I was caught up in my studies and my neuroses. In my obscure silence. My impoverished dreams. Far from him. Absent in front of him. Selfish. Unable to see.

The only thing I shared with him during these final years was his little television: he loaned it to me from time to time, when I wanted to watch something different from the rest of the family. This is my last connection to my father: a television screen.

It's sad. It's dreadful. It's horrible. But, today, I am happy to have this last connection, this wire between two stories, a pathway between the two of us. The same screen to witness the loud images of the world. News. Movies. The live broadcast of French president François Mitterrand's funeral.

It's sad, yes, sad. Somewhat beautiful?

It's all that I have left.

I am at my father's side. I have taken off all my clothing. I am still not crying. I am shouting. I am not breathing. I fall. I am crazy. I enter death. It's Friday, the holy day. It's Friday, the black day.

This is where I am, Adnane. This is where everything stops. I am stuck there forever. I have lost what came before, the father I had before. I can no longer find within myself the father from my childhood, the Mohamed from my adolescence. And this, too, is why I am writing to you. I want you to help me. I want you to come to me and tell me about that man. I want to hear your childhood memories of him, to love them and make them mine. I want to remember, through your words and your youthful recollections, my father's physical presence on earth, in this world. I want to leave this eternal moment, this incredible but true instant, this Friday morning of death. I want, not peace, but a hand—his hand, yours, Adnane—to hold and finally let the tears fall.

Would you do this for me please, Adnane, for your uncle? Would you give me a piece of your childhood, your pictures? Go with me toward that blurry, dangerous zone? Go together to the origins, ours, yours? Do you want us to continue on this voyage, to walk outside with bare feet?

You don't speak.

Don't you understand?

You must understand!

Is that a yes? Yes? Do I continue?

So I continue this letter, this walk, this moment between us three, this return, this obligation of memory.

Adnane, I've already told you but I will say it again: your skin is darker than mine and I like that. I like that you are nearly black. I like that you came from somewhere else to renew our blood, redefine our family, wear our name differently. Taïa. I like the fact that, thanks to you, the story is not going as planned.

Adnane... Did your grandfather choose that name for you? Is that true? It doesn't matter. In any case, he loved that name, he said that it came from heaven. That green name, as my mother calls it.

Adnane... You didn't exist. Now you do. You are already 16 years old.

I've just reread the last paragraph. Again I am thinking of how you came into our life. A miracle. Yes, you didn't exist. Now you do. A baby, four months old. Your parents had waited so long for you, wished so hard that you would come. They hadn't been able to conceive. They had consulted with many doctors, specialists. They despaired. They desired and they prayed.

They hadn't said anything to anyone else. They went somewhere else to find you, to the north of Morocco. Tangier? Tetouan? Nador? They brought you back. They celebrated you. We all celebrated you. We all shared in the transgression. Adoption is forbidden by Islam. We would write memory differently. I don't know if the rest of the family truly understood. Out of their love for you and for your dark skin, they disobeyed the laws.

When she first saw you, one of my sisters said: "He looks like Ahmed Zaki, the Egyptian movie star." She wasn't wrong. You bear some resemblance to that great actor.

Another shouted: "I want one, in the same color." Everyone laughed.

You brought this joy, Adnane. To your parents. To the rest of us, on your father's side and on your mother's side. Five months later, your mother got pregnant. Something was unlocked in her. A girl arrived. Imane. Your sister. My niece.

Adnane, I am only telling you all of this to share with you the meaning of your birth, of your rebirth. To affirm this moment of joy. Of cohesion. The new direction.

Adnane, you are a Taïa. You became a Taïa. As you know, this name is Arabic for "obedient." As you can't possibly know, this name has a terrible, tragic story. My father's story, above all else.

According to your grandfather's brother, we are not worthy of this name.

This uncle, who is still alive, told my father: "Our mother had you with another man. You are not a Taïa. My father is not your

(158)

father. So you have no right to any inheritance. But you can keep the name, our family name... I'll allow you to keep it."

Was my uncle telling the truth or did he create this lie to keep all the land to himself?

Mystery. Injustice. Loss.

Eternal doubt.

The truth is not important in this story.

A man was broken from the beginning and thrown into an abyss. A man was uprooted, disinherited, mocked for his whole life. They called him the "idler." They didn't look at him the way they should. They didn't see him at all.

This man is your grandfather.

His whole life long, a man lowered his eyes before his older brother who did not love him. Who scorned him.

A man wore his terrible doubt prominently, like a face, like the brand of a life. The doubt over his origins, doubt about love and its meaning. Self-doubt: Who am I? Who is my father?

This man is your grandfather.

In his endless downfall, fortunately, he discovered sex, Arabic books, and M'Barka, my mother, who made decisions for him, who cried for him, for us.

I want you to know all of this, Adnane. I want you to recognize the shame that we have endured. I hope that you too will wear our family name, Taïa, differently. That you will liberate it from the gaze of the castrating uncle. That you will reinvent it. That you will replenish it with another story, another love. And I hope that you will never forget our uncle's crime. I beg of you, don't forget. Don't turn your back on a lifetime of pain that was bravely borne for us by a man who was always smoking and dreaming.

A sentimental and silent man.

A man who I, his son, must now bring to life. To whom I must do justice. For us, you see, it will never be a question of killing the father.

Adnane... Do you understand these words? Do you grasp the hidden meaning? The love and despair that accompany them? You'll tell me... You'll write to me when you have time... I hope you will help me to once again see the images of the father I had before, with your own memories, with your juvenile strength. The happy images do exist. The timid tenderness. A moment when we looked into each other's eyes. The smoke of his cigarettes. The blessing? The salvation?

I don't want to be Ham, who was cursed by his father, the prophet Noah.

I don't want you to be Ham either, Adnane.

I dream that you will hold on to this letter for a long time, that it will serve as a point of departure for you: a text that was written primarily for you and which, in the time to come, will allow you to reflect on your life, the man you are, the man you will become more and more and whom I haven't met. Do you even have an idea of who he is, this other Adnane, this little man who is already taller and stronger than I am?

Last week, I happened upon a photo of you here, in Paris where I have been living for ten years. It was hiding amid my old files from the university. It was alone. Forgotten. Slightly yellowed.

It was the day before I left Morocco. My bedroom. The little bed in a corner. Disorder all around. On the floor, piles and piles of my movie magazines and my books that I was in the process of sorting. And in the middle, seated on the floor: you. Eight or nine years old. You smile. A big smile. You're handsome. Open. A little angel. A little devil.

What were you doing there with me? Were you helping me? Were you just watching? Was I boring you? Did you want a gift: my only Tintin album, *The Castafiore Emerald*? Maybe.

Were you sad because I was leaving?

Do you remember the moment when I took that photo? I don't.

Since last week, you and that photo are there in front of me all the time, mingled with the chaos of my thoughts, with the rhythm of my fears. This happenstance must have inspired me to write this letter, to go to you again.

Suddenly I realized that you'd grown and that I was no longer just Abdellah to you: I am your uncle from Paris. You know someone who lives in Paris. And it's me. This is not a triviality, I know. Now you must dream of Paris the way I did when I was your age. I'm sure you hope to come to Paris someday. I want to be the one who helps you realize this dream. We will do it, I promise you. You will come here. You will know me in a new light. The same Abdellah. A different Abdellah. I won't teach you anything, I won't impose anything on you. I will look at you: I will rediscover you. You will speak or you won't. You will dance or you won't. I will buy you several Tintin albums. I will buy you postcards. We'll go to the Louvre. I will take other photos of you. Maybe I'll film you. And together one evening, we will return to the story of your grandfather. And then you will need to speak… I already know: you will speak… You will help me through this crossing, this return to Morocco, to my city of Salé, my neighborhood Hay Salam, to my past in a different light. To my father who has just now died.

While we wait for this day, I only have one piece of advice to give you: be yourself in stature and in dreams… Don't let them trivialize you. Hang in there. Work. In my way, I am with you. Strength. Prayers. Affection.

Your uncle Abdellah

To Love and to Kill:
Why I Write in French

What use is the French language to me today, in 2017? In the 1980s, what mysterious reasons attracted me to a language that was anything but my own?

I am 43 years old. After having written several novels in French, I am now filled with doubt. I do not remember exactly how my sentimental and intellectual tie with the French language began. Even worse, I ask myself this question: "Do I really like that language?"

I come from a very poor world. A very large Moroccan family in the town of Salé, right near the capital of Rabat. An entirely Arabic-speaking Muslim world in which I learned the fundamentals of life: much violence and, at times, miracles of tenderness. That is all human beings like: to fight, to argue, to crush each other. I discovered that I was a homosexual in that world and, very naturally, I adopted the same survival techniques to save my skin as those around me. During my early adolescence, I invented a character for myself as a nice, polite, studious boy. I played it to perfection. Of course, this was not enough. Violence likes violence. Violence calls forth violence. I had to leave that first world which was killing me, and which I loved deeply despite it all. I had to leave it. Betray it.

Dreams, of course, are not enough. I understood this fairly quickly. Other people are always stronger. They overtake us in the end. Making fun of me again. Subjugating me again. Belittling me again.

Where is the mother whom I love so strongly? Where is the father with whom I've always stood in solidarity? Where are my older sisters, my heroines, my film stars?

At the very moment when you need other people, their tender gaze, their saving hand, you realize the bitter truth that will accompany your life forever: nobody can save any one else. Leading your own life means killing others just as they killed you. It means drying your heart. Constructing walls and barricades around yourself.

It was at that dark moment, in that terrifying solitude, that I thought the French language could save me. Carry me away, elsewhere. Far away from those people who claimed to love me and proved the opposite to me daily. The French language was a launching board, a board that would enable me to flee, to distinguish myself from others, and also to crush them.

In the head of the young adolescent that I was, that was the project. Not to love the French language, but to use it like a weapon, a technique, a precise and sharp-edged method.

With the French language I thought I would cut myself off from others. Enter into another sensibility. Another reality. A beautiful and mythical one. Arthur Rimbaud. Gustave Flaubert. Isabelle Adjani. Marcel Proust. With and through the French language I could only be free. And strong. Of course.

I knew full well that this was the language of wealthy Moroccans. The others whom we never saw, whom we never met, and who nonetheless dominated everything in the country. Just like those in power, they'd also abandoned us to poverty and ignorance. They used the French language, day in, day out, to establish a distance between us and them. Us and me. "Remain forever in that prison; do not try to lift yourselves up to our level, you shall not succeed. And you, Abdellah the dreamer, you should give up. Look at yourself. Look at yourself. Do you understand? Yes? No?"

I hated the French language spoken by those rich people. I abhorred it. But also, to be honest, I knew that I wanted the power of that language for myself. The French language as a sword to take into battle. The French language to become ruthless myself. A warrior who dares to dream and who dares to take his revenge, without a shred of doubt.

That is what I did. Not only did I eventually master that language, but I also invented myself as a writer in that language.

A writer, me! That's a mystery that will always remain complete. Something which I do very seriously and which, once the difficult work of writing is done, escapes me completely. Did I myself produce this, transform the world into words in that way? Yesterday's me? Today's me?

There is no romanticism in writing. There is nothing but vampirism. We are completely eaten up by words, by style. By what we call literature.

For the writer, there is no salvation in writing. No possible therapy. In fact, the very opposite occurs and repeats itself every time: books steal parts of your life, of your sensitivity, of your memory, of your tragedies, and then abandon you. That's how it is. That's the law. It's no use trying to fight it.

It's not schizophrenia. It's simply chaos. A greater and more generalized mess in a writer's heart. In my heart.

Today, I am living in anarchy more than ever. Over the years I've found my writing style. What comes after? It that all?

Today, I feel a great, inner dissatisfaction. As if, finally, even vengeance had no more use. I killed those who wanted to kill me. I came out on the other side, as they say. I am gay and free. I am Arabic, Muslim, and free. Really?

I arrived in Paris in 1998. I struggled to accomplish this project. To become a Parisian. I played the smartass. I belly danced for others. And I tried not to lose myself.

I had the strength, the rage, and I conquered Paris. On my own small playing field, I measured myself against this city. Paris neither impressed me nor scared me. On the contrary, in that space, in those new frontiers, I discovered the ideal terrain to try things out, to forget that I was poor, to plan my future, to shatter glass-ceilings, to fall in love with men older than myself, to break their hearts without remorse, to leave them, to forget them, never to deviate from my initial goal, never to pay attention to the ordinary racism that confronts Arabs like me.

I was 25. Now I am 43. I've placed the bulk of what I think of myself and of the world into books. I've accomplished treason and murders there. I've opened wounds and scars. I've spit rudely, vomited just as much. And one day I woke up with the aftertaste of loss. I'd lost the fight. I'd lost myself. I was lost in the streets of Paris. Lost in the West. Hating the world and hating all of this violence in myself that keeps on growing.

Anger is there, before my eyes. Nothing can quell it. Nothing.

I am but an Arab. Who speaks good French. Who writes. Who publishes. Who thinks. Congratulations, congratulations! What now? Where can I put the rest, everything that I'll never write, never say?

I can always resist the clichés that surround people like me in Paris. Arabic, Muslim, and gay. "How do you do it, my little friend? Here are our hands, bow down and kiss them as you should! Come on, a bit more submission won't do you any harm!"

I can write my anger. Feed it. Give it fire, gas, weapons.

But I'm lost. In Paris 2017. More than ever, I'm surrounded by doubt, about everything, at times about the past, about the language that I master and that doesn't love me back, about the French language. I ask myself this question every day: "Should I go back to my first language, Arabic? Write in Arabic? Pursue this operation of baring myself, in my original skin? Would this give me back a taste for life, against its limits that have become once again too reductive, in Rabat, in Paris, in New York and elsewhere."

Where to go?

I wrote that brief sentence in several of the short stories that I composed in Paris between 1999 and 2004 (translated in the book that you are holding in your hands). At the time, writing took place within me with an absolute desire for conquest. To continue the battle with nothing if not the power of despair and incessant humiliations. At the time, although I did not know it, literature allowed me to resist the Western gaze placed on people like me. It allowed me to steer clear of traps and not to enter the prison that France had prepared for me so long ago.

I was moving through Paris. Ambitious. An arriviste. Hopeless. But with an unshakeable faith in the future awaiting me, and whose glass ceilings I kept shattering.

I was erring and did not deviate from my goal.

Today, I am like that character played by Robert Mitchum in Charles Laughton's *The Night of the Hunter*. A murderer who has just been released from jail and is chasing innocent children to kill them. I am evil. Hatred. First, the entire world rejects you. Then it gives you freedom like a monumental slap in the face. It abandons you once again. You must then reconstruct everything alone, absolutely alone.

ABOUT THE AUTHOR

Abdellah Taïa (born in 1973) is the author of six novels, including *Salvation Army* and *An Arab Melancholia*, both published by Semiotext(e), and Infidels. His novel *Le jour du roi*, about the death of Morocco's King Hassan II, won the 2010 Prix de Flore. He also directed and wrote the screenplay for the 2013 film adaptation of *Salvation Army*.

You must write everything alone.

I am at the same time Robert Mitchum and the children he is getting ready to sacrifice.

Maybe writing helps those who read books. But it's useless for the crazy writer who still believes in words, even when they've been emptied of their substance. Its only use is to provide a keen consciousness of the horrible world in which, at the end of the day, we learn but one thing: how to hurt others, again and again.